To Jack and Myrna,

all the best!

David M. Quinn

LEVIATHAN'S MASTER

The Wreck of the World's Largest Sailing Ship

DAVID M. QUINN

D0126445

iUniverse, Inc.
New York Bloomington

Leviathan's Master
The Wreck of the World's Largest Sailing Ship

This is a work of historical fiction. While the author has attempted to be
faithful to the known history of persons and events, their portrayal, their
actions and words are, of necessity, creations of the author's imagination.

iUniverse books may be ordered through booksellers or by contacting:

iUniverse
1663 Liberty Drive
Bloomington, IN 47403
www.iuniverse.com
1-800-Authors (1-800-288-4677)

ISBN: 978-1-4401-5535-2 (pbk)
ISBN: 978-1-4401-5537-6 (cloth)
ISBN: 978-1-4401-5536-9 (ebk)

Library of Congress Control Number: 2009934924

Printed in the United States of America

iUniverse rev. date: 8/17/2009

The Thomas W. Lawson (1902–1907)

To Halbert W. Dow (1893–1973), beloved grandfather, who first related to me the story of his uncle, Captain George W. Dow, and the doomed voyage of the *Thomas W. Lawson*.

They that go down to the sea in ships, that do business in great waters; these see the works of the Lord, and his wonders in the deep. For he commandeth, and raiseth the stormy wind, which lifteth up the waves thereof, they mount up to heaven, they go down again to the depths; their soul is melted because of trouble, they reel to and fro, and stagger like a drunken man, and are at their wit's end.

(Psalm 107, Verses 23–27)

To the Reader

One summer when I was a boy of perhaps fourteen years, I accompanied my grandparents on a day's outing up the southern coast of Maine. At lunchtime, we stopped at a little restaurant specializing in lobsters, clams, and other such fare. As we waited for our food to be prepared, my grandfather noticed photographs on the walls depicting old-time ships and coastal scenes. He left the table and went to inspect them more closely.

After a few minutes, he called me to his side and pointed to one such photo. "That's the *Thomas W. Lawson*," he said. "My uncle was the captain of that ship." It was then that I heard the amazing story of the largest sailing ship ever built, the seven-masted schooner, and its captain, George W. Dow.

In his 2006 book, *The T. W. Lawson: The Fate of the World's Only Seven-Masted Schooner*, author Thomas Hall gives, in superb detail, a factual account of the *Lawson's* construction, final voyage, shipwreck, and rescue. I have chosen to write the story as historical fiction, from the point of view of the man at the center of this tragic adventure—my maternal great-great-uncle, George W. Dow.

Some may observe that a pattern is emerging in my writing. My first work of historical fiction, entitled *It May Be Forever: An*

Irish Rebel on the American Frontier, was an account of the life of my paternal great-great-uncle, Michael Quinn. I hope that I do not run out of interesting ancestors, whose stories reveal so much about America and the people who helped build her.

Note: Writing a nautical tale, of necessity, involves the use of certain words that may not be familiar to many readers. To remedy this issue, I have included a glossary at the back of the book.

The year 2007 marked the 100th anniversary of the loss of the *Thomas W. Lawson*. To commemorate the occasion and those who died, a memorial granite bench was placed in the churchyard on St. Agnes Island, where the recovered bodies are interred. Thomas Hall and descendants from families involved in the story, on both sides of the Atlantic, joined in sponsoring this tribute.

Courtesy of Mr. Tom Hall

Acknowledgments

My task in researching *Leviathan's Master* was greatly expedited by Thomas Hall of Scituate, Massachusetts, who generously shared much of his research material and photo images with me. I am also indebted to William Turner, distant cousin and great-grandson of Captain George W. Dow, who kindly shared details of family history and lore.

In 1998, my wife and I visited the Isles of Scilly and on that occasion were greatly assisted by Mr. Osbert Hicks, whose father was a member of the *Slippen* crew.

Thanks also go to Lois C. Johnson of Hancock, Maine, who has generously shared genealogical data and insights into the Dows of Hancock. As a member of the Historical Society of the Town of Hancock, she was good enough to contribute antique postcard images found herein.

My editor, Kathryn Agrell, has again contributed her formidable talents to the improvement of my written work. Any residual flaws are my responsibility alone.

Over the years, my family has collected numerous photos of the ship *T. W. Lawson*. Reconstructing just who made the acquisition and from what source has proved to be difficult, if not impossible. Of necessity, several of these photos appear without credit.

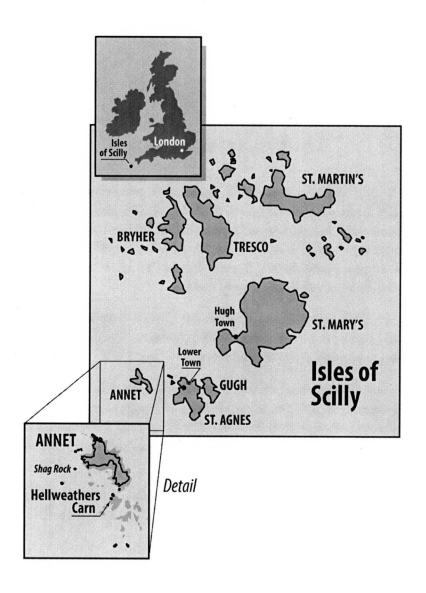

Chapter One

December 27th, 1907

Balm of Gilead, my body hurts! I lie gingerly, careful to make no sudden movements. Taking a deep breath sends flashes of pain through my sides. It even hurts when I speak. For almost two weeks, I have not walked a step. Dr. Brushfield comes now and again from the main island of St. Mary's. Says I'm better off than Mr. Rowe, whose kneecaps are smashed. They will plague him for the rest of his life. My broken ribs and broken wrist, though they vex me sorely, will heal in time. I know Brushfield's right, but I'm not greatly consoled.

The bedroom where I am confined is pleasant enough, though the bed is not quite as large as I'd prefer. Opposite the door, there is a series of three casement windows from which I am able to take the morning sun and catch a welcome glimpse of the ocean. In front of the windows, there is a stuffed easy chair, its fabric sorely faded from direct sunlight. Though I am bedridden now, I look forward to that chair. A small table beside my bed holds a kerosene lamp, my water glass, and a small potted plant that I cannot identify. Having lost all my belongings, I make little use of the simple clothes cupboard. I enjoy the familiar scent of salt air that permeates my quarters.

Mrs. Hicks, Charlotte, is an angel, floating in and out of my room, seeing to my needs. She is careful in her ministrations to avoid causing more pain for me. And she patiently bears the indelicate tasks imposed by my immobilized frame of 250 pounds. Short and somewhat matronly for her age, she nevertheless moves with grace and kindness. I like her soups, which she serves frequently, as I am unable to cut up solid fare. Frankly, I'd welcome a drop of old Jack, at least to ease the pain. But there's been no offer of spirits—even on Christmas Day!

I often see the man of the house as he passes my window, going to and coming from his work as a sailmaker and farmer. I would guess Israel Hicks is in his early forties, a tall fellow as the locals go. His brown hair is cropped very close, and a drooping, brown mustache decorates an otherwise plain and serious face. When he visits my room, he is polite, but I find his manner cool. He doesn't say much. I know he was among the lifeboat crew that brought Rowe and me to safety. Must be thinking: how does this fellow, George Dow, a well-experienced master, lose the largest sailing ship in the world? Though the coroner's jury laid no blame, I'm sure the loss of the local pilot sticks in Israel's craw.

I haven't spoken with Rowe yet. He's laid up in a room on the other side of the house. I don't care to see him just now. He's a good engineer, and I certainly harbor no ill will toward the young man. Indeed, I'm delighted that somebody survived besides me. I just don't want to talk to anyone about the wreck of the *Lawson*. Still, little else crosses my mind.

I'm on the little island of St. Agnes, in the Isles of Scilly, which is a part of Cornwall and off the southwest coast of England. From my window, the island appears as a bare, open space. All these islands are flanked with rocky shoals and ledges, creating what I've been told is a ships' graveyard. Would that I'd known that two weeks ago—though wind and weather might still have rendered me powerless to avoid the hazards of the Scillies.

The Hicks have four children, who are friendly and well behaved—a pleasant reminder of my own sons and daughter. Sadly, I don't see much of the Hicks's youngsters. They are away most of the time, to the school on the largest island. Rather than commute each day, all the children of these islands board on St. Mary's from Monday till Friday. This frees the bedrooms for Mr. Rowe and myself, though the children must be squeezed in on the weekends.

The Hicks's stone and mortar house, with its slate roof, sits on the side of a grassy hill in Lower Town, overlooking Broad Sound. The building appears to have been constructed in stages, one addition upon another. Rowe is staying in the last of these, while I am quartered in the oldest section of the building. At night, I can hear the surf crashing against the rocky shore below. This has always been a welcome and comforting sound. Now I am disturbed by its call. It laughs; it rebukes me. I, who rode the seas with taut reins for nearly fifty years, am now reproached.

Courtesy of the Gibson Family Collection
The house of Israel and Charlotte Hicks

In my memory, there is always the sea—swelling, rolling, and lapping at rocks grizzled with barnacles or bearded with deep-green, mossy seaweed. Some days, the ocean flashes firelike in the eastern dawn. On others, she lies quiet in cool sea smoke. She can be blue and inviting or steel gray and full of threats. But I never viewed the ocean as friend or foe. Though nearly as essential to our lives as the air we breathed, she was a fact of nature, and I took my sustenance from her.

In these long, confining days, my mind races back to coastal Maine and my youth. I see the nearly barren landscape, pocked acres of tree stumps for miles inland, scavenged by the shipbuilders' appetite for timber.

I think of the small family farm in Tremont, on Mount Desert Island, where I was born. It was my grandfather's place, lying on the western shore between Seal Cove and Pretty Marsh Harbor. He worked it together with his sons: Charles, Samuel, and my father, William Henry Dow. When I was eight, Father and Samuel each purchased farmland in North Hancock, selecting adjacent plots just above the Skillings River. Farms in coastal Maine are an avocation, yielding more rocks than crops. While our new farm was larger and somewhat more fertile than the Tremont farm, it would never be enough. To supplement their incomes, Father and my uncles entered the shipping trade. When Father wasn't home on the farm, he was master of the schooner *Fulcrum*.

Dow Family Photo

George W. Dow
1847–1919

I cannot recall much about Mother's folk, the Obers. My mother, Naomi, was a short, slight woman with prematurely gray locks always pinned up into a tight bun. By God, she was strong! Years of hard work on her father's farm gave her that strength, which preserved her through nine live childbirths and a stillborn. She was not given to idle talk, but she combined a loving disposition with strict discipline. When I doze off in these quiet afternoons, I can still hear her singing softly to herself, as she often did as she went about her many chores. She managed our farm capably during Father's lengthy absences, making no fuss about carrying burdens shouldered by menfolk at neighboring farms. Not like my Jennie, who rues each year I spend chasing a tailing wind.

Damn! I try to shift from one hip to the other and pain shoots through me like an electric charge. But I can't abide lying in one position for hours at a time. So, it's pick your poison. When the pain subsides, I take a sip of water and return to my reverie.

Courtesy of the Historical Society of the Town of Hancock, Maine.
Schooner under tow in the narrows between Hancock and Sullivan, Maine

I see myself as a boy, weeding and hoeing the vegetable garden, pulling an unending store of stones from our fields, fetching wood and water, milking the cow, feeding the chickens, and collecting the eggs. What a relief it was to be able to attend the little school at nearby McFarland Hill! Our farm fronted the busy Ellsworth Road on the western edge of the township. Often I would stop in the midst of a chore and watch the flow of freight wagons and carriages on that road. But there was never any thought of joining that passing parade. My life was predestined. I would go to sea.

Chapter Two

"May I come in and tidy up, Captain?"

"Do come in," I answer.

Charlotte pushes the door open with her foot, her arms fully laden with the implements of the war on dust and dirt. She is wearing a faded blue smock and a kerchief covers her hair, signals of her serious intent. This will be more than a tidying up.

As I am feeling more able to move about today, I am happy to surrender the room for an hour or so. Carefully, I move from the bed to the chair by the window, a staging point from which I will make my retreat.

"My Jennie is a dedicated housekeeper, so I am trained by her to help out or move out."

"No need to leave on my account. I'd welcome the company."

Putting down her bucket of soapy water, the mop, a feathered duster, and cleaning rags, the lady of the house places her hands on her hips and looks me in the eye. "You know, Captain, that's the first mention you've made of your wife since the night they carried you through my door—you must miss her very much."

Am I blushing? I feel a flash of warmth in my cheeks at this implied rebuke, but I respond cheerfully. "Oh yes, of course I do, Charlotte. But after almost forty years of long separations, I guess it seems a bit more tolerable to me than it might to others. But I will be greatly relieved to see her again."

"She must be a patient soul," Charlotte observes as she begins to strip the bed I have just vacated.

I begin to sputter, but manage to transform it into a cough. "Well, ma'am, I don't know as I'd go that far."

She stops and raises her eyebrows at this remark. "Really, Captain, should you speak this way?"

I glance out the window, pausing to decide how forthcoming to be. But she presses me.

"Tell me about Jennie. How did you meet?"

"Well, let's see. What can I say about my wife of thirty-seven years? I'm told we first met as classmates at the grammar school, though I don't recall anything about her from those days. You see, I went to sea at the age of twelve, about the time her family settled on a farm near our own. They were from Germany."

"From Germany? So far away!"

"Yes, ma'am. She was the youngest of eight children belonging to a physician named Ernest Bush. He had come to America after some trouble with the German authorities. The nature of the dispute is a bit of a Bush family secret, but his license to practice medicine had been arbitrarily cancelled. He arrived in Maine without much more than the clothes on his back and built a practice treating the locals and their animals. In time, he arranged for his children to join him in America, his wife having been deceased."

I shift in my chair, looking in vain for a comfortable position. Noticing my discomfort, Charlotte brings a pillow to me. "Here now, lean back on this and go on with your story while I finish making up your bed."

I had thought to go to the parlor while Charlotte cleaned, but it looks like this conversation may take a while. It's not that I object to being sociable; I just feel a bit awkward sharing these personal details. Still, I welcome the distraction from my aches and pains.

"Jennie's given name is Johanna, but only her father called her that. She was friendly with my sister Julia, and it was through Julia that we became reacquainted. I was in my late teens when I rediscovered Jennie at a Fourth of July picnic in Hancock Center. I remember that day well. It had been unusually warm that spring, and there was early corn—a good addition to the lobster, clams, and cold beer. The war had been over for more than a year, and our town band played a medley of patriotic songs in honor of our soldiers.

Charlotte looks up from her dusting, "There was a war, then?"

"Ayah, a rebellion by the slaveholding states in our country. I'm afraid it was a long, bloody affair."

Charlotte nods blankly. I remind myself that she leads a rather isolated life here on St. Agnes.

"Would you say your wife was pretty?" she asked.

"I'd say so, back then. Average in height, but she was blessed with an attractive figure. She wore her brown hair long. She had a pleasant face, a strong chin, and a thin, straight nose. She smiled readily and, happily for me, didn't giggle incessantly like Julia. I remember when we were introduced. She said, with a lingering German accent, 'I'm happy to find you between voyages, Mr. Dow.'

"Well, I wasn't sure where to take our conversation. You see, Charlotte, at that time my experience with women, other than Mother and my four sisters, was severely limited. Of course, my shipmates shared with me the less-refined perspective. Once, I offended a young maid in Cuba by falling into peals of laughter at the sight of her smoking a cigar. But polite, even casual, social contact with the opposite sex was a skill I had yet to master."

"A skill you certainly acquired in later years, Captain," Charlotte interjects with a smile.

I give a slight and precarious bow from my seated position. "You are most kind, ma'am. Well, then, where was I? Oh, right! I gave Jennie my arm, and we chatted about weather and my recent voyage to Fayal, in the Azores. She gave a polite ear to my account, but I could tell her interest was fleeting. Soon, she turned the subject to domestic matters. She described for me the itinerant practice of medicine in which she sometimes accompanied her aging father. That was when I first saw her get her dander up.

"'You cannot imagine the effort required to obtain payment from some of Father's patients,' Jennie complained. Then she went on to excoriate the slackers. It gave me the clear impression that Jennie was not to be trifled with. But I didn't mind; I've always admired a strong woman.

"Still, she seemed to enjoy my company, and I guess I fell for her right off. We continued to see each other whenever I was in home port. Being apart so much drew out the process of courtship. But, that was probably all to the best. When we finally agreed to wed, I had made captain and was financially able to take on the responsibilities of marriage and family. We were married at Hancock in July 1870."

Charlotte nods approvingly. "Any children?"

"Oh, yes, ma'am. It was less than a year later that our first son, Orville, was born. Unfortunately, I was at sea at the time, but my mother and sisters were ready to assist in all the usual ways. Some master mariners happily carry wife and children with them on voyages near and far. They prefer a bit of hardship to the pain of separation. Whenever I raised the prospect of such to Jennie, she adamantly refused. 'I'll not have my son raised in the midst of dockside rogues and ruffians.'"

Charlotte, now mopping the flagstone floor, approaches, and I carefully lift my feet, one at a time, as she cleans beneath them. The pain stops my story momentarily.

"She has a poor opinion of seamen, doesn't she?" Charlotte observes.

"Well, I chose not to remind her that she had accepted as her husband a graduate of the fo'csle. I suspect it was her own sensibilities as much as it was a concern for Orville's moral formation. When the other children—Georgia, Richard, and Ellery—came along, the issue had long been closed."

Sensing my continued discomfort, Charlotte suggests that I return to my freshly made bed. This maneuver takes several minutes to fully accomplish.

"Thank you, ma'am. This is much more comfortable."

Once I'm settled, she urges me, "Please, do continue, Captain." She returns to mopping the floor.

"Faced with a growing family, I purchased a house in Ellsworth. It was a respectable, if not grand, two-story home, with a stable behind for horse and buggy. Being in Ellsworth was a convenience to me, as I was able to easily travel by steamer to Boston, my usual home port in those years. My earnings, including a modest captain's shareholding, made life comfortable for Jennie and the children."

Courtesy of the Historical Society of the Town of Hancock, Maine.

Harbor scene — Ellsworth, Maine

The cleaning of the room is finished and Charlotte plops down in the chair by the window, happy to catch her breath. She is clearly engaged in my story. Just when I think I've satisfied her, she comes up with another line of inquiry.

"It must be trying to be separated for long periods while you're at sea."

I am taken aback at this probe into my married life, but I see no reason to be guarded at this point with this woman. In a matter of weeks I'll be gone, and we're unlikely to cross paths again.

"Our life hasn't always been a smooth sail, I'll admit. I returned from each voyage to a household whose routines were not my own. We tried to accommodate each other's ways, but the joys of reunion seemed to evaporate more quickly each time. Shortly upon my return to the sea, life's familiar rhythms returned, to our mutual relief, I suspect."

Charlotte chuckles a bit at this last remark. "Oh, Captain, we are a seafaring community. Most women here are familiar with the long absences of our menfolk. It has been my good fortune that Israel has made his living right here on St. Agnes, so I haven't had to bear that burden."

I nod in acknowledgement and continue my story. "And so things proceeded till the winter of 1881. It was then that our three-year-old daughter, Georgia, was struck down by the scarlet fever."

"Oh, Captain Dow, I am so sorry." Charlotte gazes at me with eyes full of nascent tears.

Now I am at a loss for words.... Why did I volunteer this detail?... Even after all these years, I still find myself affected when this subject comes up. In a voice thick with emotion, I continue. "Thank you, ma'am. As you might guess, it was months before I arrived home to comfort Jennie and grieve our loss together. By then, Jennie's attitude had hardened and her tongue had become sharp. As we drove back to Ellsworth from the cemetery, she turned on me.

"'For most of the year, every year, I have no husband,' she said, 'and the children have no father! You're not here for the birthing and you're not here for the burying. I might as well be a widow!'"

"Well, the poor dear! You can hardly blame her for being upset."

"I know, I know!" I am not surprised at Charlotte's sympathies. "Still, the shipping trade is what I do—what I know how to do. Anyway, Jennie's arrow found its mark. I was stung and angry. I growled, 'A sea captain's wife carries a heavy burden, to be sure. But that wasn't unknown to you before we wed. I suspect there's many a threadbare housewife, clawing a poor living from a rocky little farm, who'd jump at the chance to swap places with you.'

"After that, any warmth of affection was replaced by cool civility. Jennie's focus on the children, always strong, became nearly exclusive. I decided to return to my home upon the sea. It was only when young Ellery, who was always poorly, took sick in 1883 that I left my command and remained at home for almost a year. Jennie hadn't been well herself either—never the same after that last childbirth. One year later, mercifully, Ellery passed."

Charlotte draws the corner of her apron to her eyes. "That must have been so hard for both of you—two children lost, and so young...."

"Excuse me, ma'am." I turn away. Stupid of me to be so forthcoming with a stranger! I blow my nose and take some water.

Dow Family Photo
*Captain Dow (standing), Jennie, brother Prentice,
and nephew George C. Dow*

15

Charlotte respectfully falls silent and begins to collect her things while I recover my composure. As I do so, she returns to the chair. After an awkward silence, I am ready to resume. I decide I will shift my account to less emotional aspects.

"It wasn't long after that I moved the family to the house in Melrose, a little town just north of Boston. Orville attended the Melrose high school and showed little interest in the shipping trade. But Richard, as he turned thirteen, begged me to take him on as ship's boy. I was commanding the bark *Auburndale* at the time, and I was pleased by his interest. Further, it would be my first opportunity to have a loved one aboard. But Jennie was having none of it. 'I've lost a husband to the shippers,' she said. 'Shall I lose a son as well?'

"But the lad persisted, and I overruled his mother. 'You mustn't squelch the boy's ambitions,' I said. 'If he wants a taste of the seafaring life, give it to him! He may find it's not to his liking. Who knows? But it should be his choice, not yours.'"

Charlotte waves a finger at me. "You were right to do so, Captain. One can't steer a child like he was a ship."

"Yes. Well, it was just one more stone in the wall between us. In the end, after several years at sea, Richard chose a different path. But I gave him a good education, just like my father gave me. It was sufficient for Richard's acceptance to the Massachusetts Institute of Technology!"

"I see what a trial this has been, Captain. But your wife's feelings seem natural enough. Though perhaps she could have been more accepting...."

"Jennie is basically well meaning. But when she gets stirred up over something, her mind is made up and there's no turning her aside. I'll give you one last example of her German temper. It was two years ago. Richard, having graduated with a degree in chemistry, was working in Boston. In the course of commuting from home each day, he met a young girl by the name of Annie Dinnie. It seems they rode the same bus. You may well guess that things progressed between them, as they so often do. So Richard brought her home to meet Jennie and share their desire to marry. Jennie went wild. She threw an iron stove handle at the poor lass, crying, 'My son will not marry the first girl he meets at the bus stop!' Poor Annie left in tears."

"My goodness! What a disgrace! Do you think … Will she not relent?"

"Oh, I suspect they'll marry eventually. Richard is a strong-willed fellow. Jennie will have to accept it. But that wife of mine sure has a wicked temper."

Charlotte stands to leave, her chores and my story now completed. "Well, so it seems," she remarks awkwardly. "Now then, your room is as it should be, Captain. It's been a most interesting visit. I'll call you when dinner is ready."

She collects her things and leaves me. I can hear her muttering all the way down the hall.

Chapter Three

I can't seem to fall off to sleep tonight. I guess it was that chat with Charlotte. It's got me reminiscing again after snuffing the lamp. My mind wants to play again scenes from days past. Am I trying to confirm some artifacts of conscience? This mental wandering is beyond my control; the thoughts simply occur and recur.

Presently, I am caught up in a memory of events from back in 1884. I had been the master of the schooner *Stampede* for over seven years, shipping out of Boston. I even had a captain's share in the vessel. Then Calvin Peck, the former Hancock County tax collector, bought out all the owners of *Stampede*. He asked me to stay on as captain, and I agreed. I worked for him until Ellery's condition worsened. Then, several months after Ellery's death, I needed a new command. I set off to apply to J. S. Emery & Co., a Boston ships' broker.

Courtesy of the Peabody Essex Museum, Salem, Massachusetts
Boston Harbor – State Street block (1870)

I did not know the Emery brothers personally, though I certainly knew of them. John and Daniel hailed from the neighboring Maine township of Sullivan, sons of the local blacksmith. John was the eldest, seventeen years senior to his brother, Daniel. They had been ship owners for some years in Maine before moving to Boston in 1857. Their ships' brokerage business grew and prospered in the years before and after the War of Insurrection. At one time, the Emerys had chartered over four hundred vessels for Atkins & Co., the sugar refiners. Of course, they owned many other vessels themselves and enjoyed a wide clientele.

It was a bright September day when I approached their offices on State Street. This was the heart of the port of Boston, just two blocks off Long Wharf and across the street from the Customs House. In those days, the wharf district was a thicket of naked masts and spars rising from the decks of ships from the nations of the world. State Street crawled with carts and clerks, stevedores and seamen. Though I was a well-credentialed master, I still felt a flutter of nerves in my gut about applying to strangers for a new command.

It had been Father's idea to call upon John Emery, figuring our shared roots in Hancock County could not hurt. It was mid-morning when I called at the aging, two-story brick structure. Upon entering, I encountered a bustling cashier's office. Its clerks were absorbed in paying off ship officers and crew. Little stacks of coinage and piles of wrinkled bills were passed beneath the grillwork to weather-beaten seamen who marked the occasion with jocular asides and greedy smiles. I caught the eye of a busy clerk and inquired for the owners. He pointed to a glass-windowed door leading to a wooden staircase. As I ascended, the aged structure squeaked with each step.

In the second-floor outer office, a pleasant but harried young man took my hat and offered me a seat. He explained that Mr. Emery was presently occupied with another visitor. I idled away my time looking around at the paintings and photographs of ships and captains that decorated the walls. The place was very warm, but apparently no one thought to open a window. After perhaps a quarter hour, the senior partner emerged from his private office, escorting his guest to the door.

I still count it among my luckiest days when I first encountered the aging John Emery. Then in his late sixties, his thinning white hair and matching side-whiskers framed a pinkish face that was jovial, yet without the roundness of corpulence. His manner was friendly and welcoming, despite the fact that we were strangers to one another. Though I had worked the port of Boston for years, I was merely one of thousands of ship captains. I could not claim a widely recognized reputation. He ushered me into his office, where we sank into leather-covered armchairs bestride a little serving table. Promptly, the fellow from the outer office arrived with coffees on a tray and just as quickly retreated.

Mr. Emery handed a cup to me. "So, you're one of the Dows of Hancock. I know of your family. Good masters, as I recall. Let's see, William is your father and Charles and Samuel your uncles? When I received your letter I had you confused for another mariner named George W. Dow."

This statement caught me with a mouthful of the bitterest coffee I had ever tasted. I forced myself to swallow quickly, hiding my distaste as best as I could.

"Ayah, that happens to me all the time, sir. He's from Prospect and is some years my senior. I've not met him, though I understand we're distant cousins."

"Ah well, if you've inherited the reliability and good character of your family, you'll do well in the shipping trade. Tell me, have you handled other than schooners in your day?"

I was well prepared for this line of inquiry, having rehearsed the details many times.

"I've served on and commanded brigs and barks, but mostly schooners," I admitted. I then proceeded to give a brief account of my career as seaman, mate, and then captain. Emery nodded and seemed satisfied. He turned abruptly to a discussion of the state of the shipping business.

"You know, George, when Dan and I first came down here, those were the glory days. American vessels and their masters dominated the U.S. foreign trade. I think it was because our captains were fully responsible for soliciting cargo, negotiating rates, and clearing customs—besides managing their ships. Our European competitors, mostly the British, simply provided transportation and could not deal on behalf of their shippers. As a result, we beat the pants off them, commercially speaking."

Emery basked in contemplation of that halcyon period. He sipped his coffee, brave fellow, and then shifted into a more subdued tone.

"After the war, things began to change. The Brits had given their masters comparable powers. They also began to build steamships and iron-hulled vessels. Our previous advantages in New England with wooden shipbuilding became increasingly irrelevant. Our major foundries are located near coal and iron deposits, too far inland to support shipbuilding. Now, American-flagged vessels haul less than 20 percent of our country's international cargo."

The old man cast his gaze to some point across the room, becoming lost in his thoughts. This period of silence I found uncomfortable. I waited and waited, then cleared my throat and interjected, "And yet, your company does a very good trade, it seems. I've spoke many an Emery vessel bound for the Caribbean, South America, or Africa. I'd like very much to serve in the Emery fleet, should a command become available."

John's face regained its former glow. "Right," he said. He rose and walked over to his large, cluttered desk. He picked up a black bound ledger and flipped through its pages. Then, marking his place with his index finger, he turned to me. "There may be such a position ... a bark called the *Gem*. She's a bit long in the tooth, built in '61. But we overhauled her last year and she will serve well for some time to come."

In my enthusiasm I stood, happily setting my nearly full cup on the tray. "I'd be grateful for the opportunity, sir. Sometimes it's the older vessel that performs best—all the kinks worked out by her masters and through refitting."

He approached me and took my arm in his. "Let's go next door. I'd like you to meet Dan. Let's see if we can't settle this today."

Where John was warm and welcoming, Dan Emery was polite yet cautious. He looked nothing like his brother. He was a heavier man, with thinning hair and bushy eyebrows. He, too, questioned me about prior service and former employers. To my relief, an offer was agreed.

Dow Family Photo

Captain Dow on the deck

I emerge from this half-sleep, half-dream. The moonlight from the window lights the room well. I grapple for the bedpan, choosing the discomfort of movement over the discomfort of needing to piss. Once that is done with, I can lie back and relax, hoping for true slumber. It doesn't happen. Inexorably, I slip back into the memory left hanging from before.

The *Gem* would be my first command within the Emery fleet, though not the last. After two years, I was assigned the schooner *Albert L. Butler*, another older but refitted vessel. My longest tenure, and favorite command, was as master of the *Auburndale*, a bark I commanded from 1891 till 1905. From that first day, my relationship with the Emerys was everything I might have hoped. And John was like an uncle to me. There were occasions, usually around Christmas, when Jennie and I would be among the guests of John and his wife, Prudence, at their home on Concord Square.

I had great respect for Daniel, and he always treated me fairly. But after John passed away in 1895, the joy of my association with J. S. Emery & Co. went with him. I had truly grown to love that old man.

In 1902, I was still with the Emery Company when the *Thomas W. Lawson* was launched. Call it a sailor's curiosity, but I wanted to see that leviathan—over four hundred feet long, tip to tail, with seven masts towering 193 feet high. When invited by John Crowley, I jumped at the chance. Anyone who was someone in shipping would be there. From my years of sailing out of Boston, I knew John and his brothers Arthur and Elmer. Together they ran the Coastwise Transportation Company that, along with Mr. Lawson, was a principal owner of the vessel.

Taking the train to Quincy in the heat of July, Jennie and I joined the thousands attending the launch ceremony. It was sunny, hot, and muggy. Thank God, there was cold beer. The Fore River Ship and Engine Company was the builder of the *Lawson*. Their founder and superintendent was Thomas A. Watson, famous for his assistance to Alexander Graham Bell. Anyway, shortly after two in the afternoon, Watson's daughter, Helen, slapped the bow of the giant schooner with a bottle of champagne. Down the skids the great ship went, colors hung and pennants flying. The crowd was cheering and a band playing. Lordy, that vessel was immense—a beautiful sight! Little did I imagine that, five years later, I would succeed Arthur Crowley as master of the bloomin' thing.

Helen Watson christens the Thomas W. Lawson
July 10, 1902

The *Lawson* was named for financier, copper speculator, and President of Bay State Gas Thomas W. Lawson. Just like the proud s.o.b. to name the largest sailing ship in the world after himself! She was built to compete economically with steamers, relying on wind rather than devoting a third of her hold to coal to fire boilers. And by using steam-driven donkey engines to raise sails and anchors, the crew size could be reduced from forty seamen to less than half that number.

Sounded good on paper! But the ship's design was later discovered to be somewhat flawed. Metal-hulled vessels proved to be bottom light compared to their wooden predecessors. And because of her immense size, the *Lawson* also presented a huge amount of free board to the wind, making her unstable unless fully loaded. She was difficult to maneuver, and tacking her in the face of a headwind could be painfully slow.

Lastly, her draft of thirty-two feet meant the only Atlantic port deep enough to accommodate her was Newport News, Virginia. Still, she was a marvelous vessel when fully loaded and running before a strong wind, passing even powerful steamships with ease. And she had electric lighting and steam-heated fo'csle and stateroom.

The Thomas W. Lawson under tow

The Crowleys ran her as a coastal collier for four years before having her refitted as a bulk liquid carrier. Then, pulled by a tugboat and with topmasts removed, she carried oil from Port Arthur, Texas to Pennsylvania under a lease to the Sun Oil Company. When the folks at Sun proposed using the *Lawson* for Atlantic crossings, the Crowleys balked. They knew the *Lawson* might have trouble with such a voyage, given her design problems.

I had left the employ of the Emerys and command of the *Auburndale* late in 1905. I felt I needed to be home with Jennie in those days, her health being a concern from time to time. Our younger son, Richard, had been living at our home in Melrose. But at the age of twenty-six, he would not long be happy with that. Though I missed being at sea, I was not really looking for a new command. I had partnered with my brother-in-law in an agricultural implements business down in Ellsworth.

Then, early in 1907, Arthur Crowley telephoned. I hadn't seen him in several years, and I was taken aback when he asked to come calling. I figured Coastwise wanted my services, though I never suspected it might be for the *Lawson*. I suggested he come after dinner, as Jennie would be napping. No need to get her riled up before any decision was taken.

Captain Crowley was a thickset fellow in his late thirties, with closely cropped, light hair. A shadow of a mustache was the only hint of whiskers on his face. He was fourteen years junior to his brother John, yet he looked twenty years older than his years. When he came in, he seemed less than comfortable. I presumed it was the dismal weather. It seemed to me it might snow that evening. We sat in the parlor, nursing hot tea against the cold and winter gloom outside. Despite the hour, I burned the electric lights.

"John would have come, George, but he's down with a hacking cough," Arthur began. "He usually handles the management side, while Elmer and I command vessels." He shifted in his chair without finding his ease.

I pretended not to notice and busied myself with loading my pipe. "Tell John I wish him a speedy recovery. These winter colds are a nuisance! But don't fret, Arthur. Whether it's you or John, it's shipping that's the subject at hand. What can I do for you?"

Arthur cleared his throat. "Well, George, we'd like you to take command of the *Lawson*."

I was speechless. I stood and made a fuss of brushing bits of tobacco off my vest. Then, with a laugh, I said, "What's the matter, Arthur? You getting tired of being hauled up and down the coast by a steam tug? I wouldn't blame you at all. Nearly makes a passenger out of a fine captain like yourself. No, don't try to sell such a post to me."

Arthur placed his cup on the side table. His face had visibly reddened. "Oh, it ain't the coastal run for the *Lawson*, George. The folks at Sun Oil want to deliver kerosene to London. You'd have her under sail, good and proper."

I froze at the mention of London just as I went to strike a match. "London! The *Lawson's* never been an open-sea carrier —might never be with her hard-luck reputation."

Crowley jumped to his feet; then, apparently embarrassed at his reaction, he resumed his place on the settee. He seemed to me afraid. Maybe he was worried that no master worth his salt would take the position.

"Now, hold on, George! That's a lot of seadog hooey. Sure, she's run aground on occasion, but she was never built for the coastal trade. She'd have been a deep-water vessel save for the damned international manning regulations. But those requirements are behind us. The *Lawson* can sail the oceans and turn a good profit too. I tell you, George, she'll handle well, loaded and in open waters."

I stared at the carpet, my mind racing. I needed time to digest this crazy notion. I turned back to Crowley. "If it's true what you say, why aren't you happy to take her across?"

Crowley shifted again. "You know I'm a coastal man—always have been. You've been a deep-water master since before I was born! Besides, John wants a man who knows schooners back and forth, inside and out."

"When's the sailing? She'll need refitting, top-masts replaced, new rigging."

"I'm not clear on that yet. But you're right. We'll refit her in New York. Can't say how long that will take. I would guess we're looking at August or September, maybe."

As he stood to leave, he pressed me for an answer.

"I'll give it serious thought," I promised, fetching his coat and hat. "Tell John I'll have an answer for you in a day or two. You know I have a high regard for you Crowleys. With John Emery gone and Dan easing away from the brokerage, I can't think of a company more to my liking. But it's the ship, you see. It's that oversized 'tin can' that's the worry."

Arthur didn't push further. He thanked me, we shook hands, and he passed out into the gathering dusk.

August or September, eh? At least the weather ought to be tolerable.... Jesus, what will Jennie say?

Chapter Four

January 9th, 1908

"Captain Dow, a gentleman's come on the ferry from St. Mary's to see you," Charlotte informs me shortly after clearing away the leavings from breakfast. Though I am fully dressed, I lie on my bed, where I am still most comfortable. I watch the nasty weather outside my window. There is rain to beat the band. Bad time to come calling!

I am leery. "Who is he?" I have no wish to waste more time and energy with that fool from Atlantic Mutual, the insurer of our cargo.

Charlotte wipes her wet hands with her apron and, as if imparting a state secret, whispers, "I've not seen this one before—a young man with a London accent. I can always tell them's from London."

I nod and wave her away. Two minutes later, the visitor stands at my door dripping, a sodden leather valise in hand. I can smell the damp on his clothing. The light of the oil lamp catches droplets of rain in his dark, curly hair, suggesting a kind of a halo. He looks a bit green in the gills to me, but he manages a weak smile.

"Captain Dow, good day to you, sir. Thank you for your time—"

I interrupt. "Not much of a day if you ask me. And don't thank me before we've settled on a topic that's agreeable. What business brings you out in such weather, young man?"

He casts an eye about the room, seeking a place to settle himself. He seems a bit unsteady.

"My name is Francis Dagenham," he says as water pools at his feet. "I'm a correspondent from the *Times* of London. I was hoping we might have a visit and discuss the circumstances of your voyage … and its tragic end."

Carefully, I shift my position. I try to mask my discomfort, but not my displeasure.

"That's last month's news, my friend. The coroner's report was fully covered by the British press. Surely, your readers have moved on since then."

"If you please, Captain Dow, might I sit? I'm afraid the seas were rather wild on the crossing from St. Mary's. I've a bit of *mal de mer* just now."

I point to the chair by the window. "I won't begrudge a man respite from the elements," I allow. "Not used to being tossed about, eh?"

Sheets of rain stream down the windowpanes. Gusts of wind rattle the casements repeatedly. Charlotte appears at the door again and enters cautiously with a tray of hot tea and fixings.

"Just listen to that weather! This will warm you, mister."

She places the tray on my table and, with a hint of a curtsy, says to the visitor, "If you'll help the captain to a cup, I'll leave you gentlemen to your business." With Dagenham's ready assent, she exits, closing the door behind her.

I study the man as he pours our cups of tea. Despite his half-drowned appearance, he is rather handsome, in a manly way. Despite his ingratiating smile, there is something about him—maybe his piercing gaze—that suggests he is no fool.

"Now, tell me why I want to rake over the coals of the *Thomas Lawson*."

Dagenham sits again and mops his face with his handkerchief, apparently relieved to be off his feet. He positions the valise beside the chair and summons a reply.

"You are correct, sir. The sinking was fully reported at the time, and the coroner's inquest as well. But these were matters of commerce interrupted, of legal procedure running its course. I've come to find the human face of the story. It is my intention to recount for our readers the drama of the crisis and the bravery of those involved."

I scratch at my unshaven chin, repressing an oath that would not endear me to Charlotte, were she within earshot.

"Pshaw! Bravery? Drama? You make it sound like a playhouse trifle, something served up to an ogling, gullible audience. Why should I subject the good names of honest seamen to exaggerated heroics or casual ridicule? They deserve better than to be a source of amusement for the idly curious!"

The reporter doesn't mount an immediate defense. He shakes his head sadly as if wounded by misguided criticism. He places the valise back on his lap.

"Would you be offended, sir, if I should steady my stomach with a modest dram of spirits?"

With that he extracts from the valise a scarcely opened bottle of what appears to be whisky of the Scottish variety. He looks at me solicitously.

"I'd only be offended, young man, if you indulged in a solitary fashion, without the good grace of sharing."

I carefully reach for the cup of tea at my bedside and pour its remaining contents into the potted greenery Charlotte has provided to make my quarters more cheery. Dagenham smiles and serves me a generous dram of whisky. Then he takes his cup of tea and spikes it with a dollop. In time, we are engaged in animated conversation. My misgivings about being interviewed are measurably diminished.

"I'm sorry to hear you won't be visiting London," Dagenham says. "I'm sure my editors would be most welcoming, and the city is full of wonderful landmarks."

I wipe my drooping mustaches. "What makes you think I'm a stranger to London? Why, I made my first visit there as a lad of sixteen years."

Dagenham sips his drink slowly and begs me for details. He seems genuinely intrigued to learn of my youthful exploits.

"After all, one isn't born a sea captain," he presciently observes.

I punch at my pillow for improved support and begin, "I shipped with my father for several years as cabin boy. We made voyages to the Caribbean, but the War of Insurrection ruined the coastal trade. Many of our Yankee merchantmen were lost to Confederate cruisers. In 1864, my Uncle Willis, also a master mariner, approached Father with the offer of a seaman's job for me. Both Mother and Father were rather dubious. I'd served well, Father admitted; I was due my seaman's post. But, there was the danger."

The room seems noticeably quieter. The rain has stopped pounding the roof and windows, though the gusts of wind continue.

"The storm's letting up a bit, I think."

"Good job, that," Dagenham says with a note of relief in his voice. "I'll be able to get back to St. Mary's on the afternoon ferry."

"Right!" I nod, holding out my empty cup. "So, Willis, he was Father's younger brother. He had several contracts, one of which was to deliver oranges and lemons from the port of Palermo in Sicily to Boston. He assured my parents that his route across the Atlantic would skew north, initially, to avoid enemy vessels. It was late in the spring, so the seas ought not be too rough. In the end, it was agreed. We shipped out of Boston in mid-May.

"We were only out a couple of days when we were becalmed in a fogbank east of Newfoundland. As there was no wind, I was given a ditty bag and put to maintenance tasks about the rigging. The second morning, the wind returned without warning. I was at the starboard rail coiling some lines when it happened. Suddenly, our sails snapped and billowed. Another seaman, arranging lines on the windward side, mistakenly released the fore and aft mainsail boom. Before he realized his error, the boom swung violently alee and smacked me across the shoulder blades, pitching me into the drink."

"Bloody hell, man, you must be joking!"

"I am not the joking kind," I snort. "'Tis the unadorned truth."

He recoils at my chastening. "Just a manner of speaking, Captain. I shouldn't doubt a word of it."

Somewhat mollified, I resume my account. "Seawater invaded my nose and mouth before I could react. The shock of the icy waters was as daggers to my body. I was able to retch the seawater with much coughing and sputtering. But my heavy, sodden coat was pulling me under. With difficulty, I wriggled out. I thought to shed my shoes but could not manage to release them."

The memory I have conjured affects me to a surprising degree. My current pains echo those of long ago. I can almost feel the penetrating cold and the burning sensation of salt water swallowed. With effort, I continue my story.

"Apparently, no one saw me fall. The return of the wind had triggered orders from the mate to trim sails and make way. Despite my desperate calls for help, the schooner passed into the lingering mist and out of earshot. I'm not a great swimmer, but I figured I could conserve my energies best by floating on my back. I did this for some time, occasionally taking a wave in the face. Repeatedly I called out, 'Man overboard!', but without result.

"I was lost and no one knew it. Or if my absence had been discovered, where might the search begin? Uncle Willis had no idea just when or where I had gone missing. I knew that soon the chill would penetrate deep into my body, immobilizing my limbs. I recalled an old psalm Father used to recite.... 'God is our refuge and strength, an ever-present help in trouble. Therefore we will not fear, though the earth give way and the mountains fall into the heart of the sea....'"

My voice trails off and I have become distracted for a moment. Dagenham waits patiently, sensing my turmoil. I take a quaff from my cup and mutter, "Sorry."

"And yet," Dagenham interjects, "you apparently made your way to England."

"Ayah. Two fishermen in a dory picked me up. They were part of a group launched from a cod ship out of Gloucester. They were working the Grand Banks and heard my calls for help. I was nearly done in when they pulled me aboard. Biggest catch of the day, they called me. In time, they put me aboard a British merchant returning to London. Before leaving, I asked the cod men to send word to my family, and they swore they would do so upon their return. Must have slipped their minds. Mother and Father were never told of my rescue."

"Rather thoughtless, I should think.... So, that's when you visited London. Was it difficult to get return passage?"

"I crewed with three different merchantmen, working my way home through Bombay, Singapore, and Rio de Janeiro. I landed in New York over a year after leaving home. My wages were sufficient for me to purchase rail passage to Portland and a steamer from there."

"Your family must have been given a fine start upon your arrival back home!"

"It was Mother who saw me first, walking up the lane. She covered her mouth with both hands and sank to her knees. She must have thought I was a ghost. God knows I almost had become one."

There's a knock at the door. Charlotte pokes her head in and gently announces dinner. Dagenham admits that, as yet, he is unable to face the prospect of solid food. I make apologies to our hostess for both of us.

The reporter pulls his pocket watch and consults the time. Our visit is passing quickly and I know he wants to get on to the subject of his article. I decide to turn from this boyhood tale.

"Well now, the *Lawson* voyage, where to begin? Perhaps as I assumed command last September?" He nods enthusiastically for me to proceed.

"I left Boston at mid-month, traveling by rail to New York, where the refitting had been performed. A short-term crew had been engaged by the owners to conduct open-sea trials—"

"Sea trials for a vessel with five years of service?"

"Of course! No two ships perform exactly the same. As the new captain, I needed to gain a feeling for how she would handle in various conditions. Also, there were new topmasts placed, and the rigging and sails were new. Anyway, we returned to New York on October 12th and berthed near the Quarantine Station, alongside the *Lusitania.*"

"And you sailed from there to Philadelphia?"

"Well, actually to Marcus Hook," I correct.

"I'm sorry, sir. Marcus Hook?"

"Ayah, it's a small village on the Delaware River, north of Wilmington, but just within the state of Pennsylvania. The Sun Oil Company has its refinery and storage tanks there. We would take on over two million gallons of kerosene, filling our seven pair of holding tanks 'tween decks."

Dagenham squirms a bit in his chair and interrupts, "Excuse me, Captain. With all that liquid cargo, would not the ship's stability be endangered should the seas create a sloshing action within the hold?"

It's a better question than I might have anticipated from a news correspondent. "That's a risk the designers took into account. They created expansion trunks, smaller top sections of each tank to confine the liquid in a tighter space. These trunks also provide room for expansion of the oil due to temperature changes."

"Ingenious! Please continue, sir."

"It was early November when we arrived and loading could begin. This was rather later in the season than I had hoped, as winters on the North Atlantic can be stormy. But the refitting had been extended and thus the sea trials delayed."

The reporter scribbles rapidly in his notebook as I speak. I take advantage of his preoccupation to pause briefly and recollect the events of those difficult days.

"Securing a crew for the transatlantic voyage was not easy. The *Lawson*'s reputation of groundings and difficulty in coming about had preceded her. I convinced Bent Libby, my long-time first mate from the *Auburndale,* to come out of retirement from the sea, which he did most reluctantly. And Mr. Rowe was an original crewmember from the *Lawson*'s earliest days. But most of the crew would be what I could scrounge in New York and Philadelphia. Then just before our scheduled departure, six of these seadogs deserted. They claimed the ship was unsafe. So we were delayed three days while I hurriedly chased down replacements, such as they were."

Dagenham looks up from his writing, his eyebrows merging into a solid line. "Really, these men had premonitions of disaster?"

"Well, as I said, the *Lawson* did have a reputation. And seamen are a superstitious lot. They noticed right off that the ship's name had thirteen letters, as did the Sun Oil Company. And they may have had a point, as no sooner had we left Marcus Hook than we ran aground on a sandbar in the river. Luckily, our tug, the *Paraguay*, was able to free us promptly."

"When did you first encounter deteriorating weather?" he queries.

"The fair weather we enjoyed lasted about five days. We had taken the great circle route across the North Atlantic and were closing on the Grand Banks when the first gale hit us. The barometer dropped steadily, and strong westerly winds sent the seas into deep swells. At first, we greeted this change as good fortune. A tailing wind of this strength would deliver us to our destination in short order. But, by evening the winds were howling and the waves were towering. The *Lawson* would descend steeply into troughs so deep that the wind couldn't find us. Then as we ascended the next peak—bam! The wind would return like a hard slap across your face. The slackened sheets snapped like the crack of gunfire, and the steel mast hoops rattled a strange metallic cacophony. The crash of the waves upon our deck was like thunder. The force of the wash smashed all our life rafts and the captain's gig. It even bent and twisted the davits that held them. And so it continued for days."

I stop at this point and motion with my cup, which has gone empty at the wrong moment. Dagenham gives a sigh and sets down his pencil and notes. But he graciously complies. When he is settled again, I resume.

"Of course we had reefed our sails, but to no avail. The high winds, sometimes gusting to ninety miles per hour or more, blew out sails such that only tatters flew from most masts. The conditions were so desperate, I could not even have new sails placed, as the men would surely be carried away. Still, the heavy-laden vessel sat well; and with the enclosed wheel and chart house and steam-heated quarters, we were confident that we would weather the storm without added difficulty.

"After five days, the tempest passed us by, though the winds were still strong and the seas churning heavily. It was the morning of our twelfth day at sea. We hadn't seen another vessel since leaving the Grand Banks. Just before the first dogwatch, that's coming upon four in the afternoon in your parlance, Bent Libby—God rest his soul—came to my salon. Bent and I had been shipmates and friends for years. He was more of a son than an employee, being almost half my age. He pulled his sou'wester and reported.

"'Sir, the lowers are holding nicely, with remaining topsails furled. There's been some damage to the number 6 hatch cover, and we've taken water between hatches 6 and 7. We've mended the cover with lashed canvas for now. I got a sighting this morning and estimate our position at 48° north and a bit less than 30° west. Crew's all in from clearing suctions and strainers befouled by coal washing about the bilges. The storm's left them a bit shaken as well.'

"'And the weather?' I asked, feeling somewhat relieved to have come through without greater damage. Bent's expression was grim, his eyes shifted repeatedly.

"'I'm not happy with it, sir. The winds are still gale force, probably nine on the scale. But she veers counterclockwise and the barometer is falling again. I'm thinking that blow we weathered has a brother following.'

"I paced my salon. Oh, you should have seen it—all paneled, carpeted, lit with electric lamps, and furnished with plush, leather-covered furniture. How incongruous was this setting, in the midst of the bare forces of nature mounting outside.

Captain's salon

"'Leave a single jib and reef the lowers before the first watch. I don't want to lose any more canvas if I can help it.'

"'Aye, aye, sir. Anything else, sir?'

"'I'm glad to have you with me, Bent. Thanks for your service, once again. We've been through storms before. We'll get through this next one too!'

"'God willing, sir. Thank you, sir.'"

Poor Bent! There he was, happily employed with Armour & Co. in Boston, living the landlubber's life. Now his widow Annie and their five youngsters are left to shift for themselves.

My throat is choked up; I cannot go on. My visitor, sensing well my state of mind, stands and says, "Well, I need to break for a few minutes." I give him directions, and he wanders off to the out-building that Charlotte calls the "necessary place." I am embarrassed by these emotional displays of mine. Not like the usual me—a barnacled old salt! I pour another dram and send her to the hold. By the time he's back, I'm in possession of myself again.

When we resume, I ask, "Are you getting what you came for, young man? I hope this detail is not too much for your readers."

The reporter smiles and gently replies, "You're doing splendidly, Captain. And please, do call me Francis, sir." He tops up our drinks, discreetly ignoring the missing dram.

"Bent was right about the weather," I continue. "By the time I returned from the wheel and chart house for supper, the skies had darkened again and the winds increased. The men had reefed the mainsails as ordered. When the seventeen-year-old cabin boy, Mark Sampson, brought in my evening meal, there was sleet and snow on his cap and shoulders. A quiet, nervous demeanor had replaced his normal jovial manner. He set out the meal silently and left with only a 'Good evening, sir.'

"By morning, we were again in the midst of a terrible blow, even a bit worse than the first. As before, the waves thundered against the steel hull. Hurricane-force winds screamed through the masts and rigging, shredding sailcloth here and there. It was this last that worried me so. Without adequate canvas, we would lose way, perhaps be turned abeam the wind and waves. Crewmembers alternated between bouts of seasickness, exhaustion, and the paralysis of fear. Libby and Mr. Crocker, second mate out of New York, were challenged to keep the crew occupied, as deck duty was judged too hazardous and the automation of the ship operations left little work to be done. Only the firemen were required to stoke our boilers. My trips to the wheel and chart house were infrequent due to the severe pitching and rolling of the vessel. Still, I remained in telephone contact from my stateroom."

Dagenham interjects, "And this second gale, Captain, what was its duration?"

"Our voyage was forecasted to take fifteen days or so. It took us twenty-four. I think that second blow lasted about four days. As I recall, it began on December 1st or 2nd. Before it blew itself out, we were running with bare poles—all but six sails in tatters and those left were well furled. The winds blew us forward at such a rate. I would judge our speed at twelve knots or so—without canvas! Seamen took turns at the wheel for two-hour shifts—such was the mental effort required. They fought valiantly to keep the *Lawson* before the wind. Our days were like wakeful nightmares. Our nights were nearly sleepless. The sounds that 'tin can' made were unlike any I'd ever heard in almost fifty years at sea, in good weather or foul."

Dagenham becomes increasingly excited over the predicament of the *Lawson* and its crew. He furrows his brow, purses his lips.

"A moment, please, Captain." He stands up, I would think happy to move about after sitting so long. He paces before the window and gazes out at the darkened sky, perhaps trying to visualize the scene. With his back to me, he asks, "What was the state of mind among your crew during this period? They must have been gravely concerned."

"As I said before, this wasn't the best lot of seamen I ever sailed with. Take Miller, the steward—a nasty character without redeeming qualities. He was continually predicting imminent disaster. And the Swedes and Norwegians weren't much better, being highly superstitious. It was hard to get them moving, though Crocker did his best to encourage the men. Worst of the lot was that damned German, Bohnke. I suspected that, as soon as we touched land, he would desert the ship in an instant. If it weren't for Libby, Crocker, Rowe, and the Englishman, George Allen, we would have lost our vessel well before arriving here in the Scillies."

The winter darkness has begun to consume the late afternoon. Draining the last of my drink, I place the empty cup on the bedside table. Unfortunately, the two of us have made short work of the bottle.

"I must let you go. There's no lodging here on St. Agnes, so you'll wish to reach St. Mary's tonight."

"Yes, I mustn't miss the ferry. And I shan't wish to rush your account of the sinking."

He returns his notebook and the empty whiskey bottle to his valise. "Perhaps we can finish tomorrow?"

I rest my head back on my pillow. A warm glow is upon me; I am feeling rather drowsy. "Ayah. But don't come with an empty valise. All this yarning makes a man dry."

Chapter Five

January in the British Isles is a dark, gloomy time. The sun seems to go on holiday for most of the month. When it does appear, one must move quickly to take advantage of its fleeting presence. Such a moment occurs today. About late morning, I see Dagenham from my window where I am enjoying the unfamiliar brightness. I watch him as he climbs the path to this cluster of homes scattered about the side of the hill.

As Charlotte and Israel are out, I shuffle myself to the door and step out, hungry to feel the sunlight on my face. It's my first real venture beyond the door since I arrived. The air is still chilly despite a decent breeze from the southwest. Dagenham is breathing a bit heavily as he approaches the house.

"Good morning, Captain Dow," he puffs. "How are you feeling today?"

"I'm well enough, thanks. Charlotte is off to St. Mary's to shop, so I won't be offering tea. I'm sorry."

"Not to worry, sir." The young man lifts his valise and pats its side affectionately, as if it were a baby's stern. I smile and wave him inside. Today we'll sit in the parlor with its settee, stuffed chairs, and coal-burning fireplace. The north-facing windows provide a view of the Sound but don't provide the brightness I enjoy in my room. The furnishings are modest, and, like most Victorian furniture, they lack basic comfort. Despite this, I manage to cushion myself with the pillow from my bed. The sunlight ebbs and flows as clouds scud above the blue expanse of Broad Sound.

"You look a damn sight better today," I remark as we settle into chairs around the meager fire.

"It was a much easier voyage today. I'd have come by sooner, but I spent some time with Mr. Hicks—Israel. Met him as I left the quay." He pulls his notebook and pencil from his case. I crane my neck to see if he'll pull anything else, but he doesn't. I decide to be patient; it is only mid-morning.

Flipping pages in his notebook, Dagenham begins. "I thoroughly enjoyed yesterday's chat, despite my physical distress. Let's see … You were in the midst of the second gale.… Yes, you had just told me of your crew, some of whom were a bit frightened and balky."

"Right. That second gale passed us by, as did the first. The seas were still rolling wildly, but the sense of panic among the crew subsided a bit. There were additional hatch covers blown, and we set about to pump the bilges as best we could. I ordered a new jib put out to help us maintain a course. The wind pushed us well enough without other canvas.

"As the skies were low and thick, there was no opportunity for a sighting. I guessed our position to be about 150 miles southwest of Ireland's Mizzen Head but had no way to be certain. I felt like the captain of a floating bottle, entirely at the mercy of the wind and currents. Still, I had my compass, and attempted to stay well off the Irish coast."

Dagenham interrupts, "The coroner's report mentioned a third gale. That would be the storm that struck us so hard in England, indeed in all of Western Europe, from Sweden to Portugal. Our paper reported inland flooding, telegraph poles down, trees uprooted, chimneys toppled—even a small earthquake in France. Three other vessels were reported lost beside your own."

"I can't say I'm surprised. I've seen foul weather in my day, but three gales in succession? This last struck us on the tenth. The barometer fell again and the winds returned to hurricane force. Rain and sleet alternated, icing the deck and poles, then washing them clear again. I told Bent to set lookouts at fore and abeam so that we might heave to before running aground. That order remained in effect till the thirteenth, when we spotted what we thought to be a ship off the starboard bow. It was only when the low clouds partially lifted that we recognized it as a lighthouse, not a ship's mast."

"Did you realize you were in the Scilly Isles and dangerously exposed?"

I shake my head, recalling the mix of relief and confusion I felt that day. We had found landfall, but where? And we still had this major storm at our back.

"Not immediately," I reply. "Only after consulting my charts did I confirm my position and the lighthouse as Bishop's Rock. As we could see breakers dashing against the rocks and ledges, I quickly ordered our two five-ton anchors deployed—150 fathoms on the port side and 90 on the starboard. The wind was west-southwest and blowing about twenty-five knots. Heavy rollers continued to threaten us before Annet Island. But my anchors were tethered with 2 ¾-inch steel stud-link chain. I believed our ship safe enough until a tugboat could be arranged. We saw a flare rocket fired, so the locals knew of our presence."

Dagenham riffles back in the pages of his notebook. "Mr. Hicks ... he was at the quay this morning. ... Though he wasn't present that night, he related a second-hand account of the dispatch of the lifeboat, *Charles Deere James*. That's the boat that brought the pilot out. They left St. Agnes about 4:00 that afternoon. He said the weather was very dirty, and the crew got wet, cold, and fatigued with rowing even before reaching open waters where a sail might be safely raised. Still, once they cleared Annet, the winds and waves hit with full force, causing the craft to take on water. Only their deep knowledge of those perilous waters allowed them to avoid the ragged shoals along their course."

"Ayah, we watched them as they approached. It was about five in the evening when they came into view."

Dagenham smiles. "Israel also said the *Lawson* looked like a picket fence to his mates, with all those masts.... But a closer look revealed the extensive damage sustained in the course of these storms."

"We were a nasty sight." I pull the pipe that Dr. Brushfield brought me and proceed to load it with tobacco. "Anyway, the *Charles Deere James* hailed us as they came abeam our starboard rail. 'Do you know where you are?' the coxswain called, shouting above the wind.

"I assured him that I was aware of my position. He replied that I was in most dangerous waters. I told him I was all right. But he insisted, 'Sir, you are not all right.'

"I shouted back, 'My anchors are out.... They have held me well in the past.' But he would have none of it and urged me to get underway or abandon my ship."

Dagenham leans forward, a furrowed brow upon him. "Did you seriously consider that invitation to abandon ship?"

"My friend," I reply between puffs as I light up, "a master does not easily take a decision to abandon his ship and cargo. I noticed that the tide had turned and believed the worst was over, despite the increasing winds. Besides, my crew was played out for lack of sleep, my ship was damaged, and I had no sails with which to maneuver. I could only stay put till morning."

"How was it that the pilot came aboard?"

"I suspect the coxswain had exhausted his powers of persuasion. We could see them as they argued back and forth among themselves as to whether someone should come aboard and who that should be. Apparently, there were several qualified Trinity House pilots on the *Charles Deere James*. In the end, only Billy Cook proved willing. Anyway, he shouted for permission to board."

"Can you describe pilot Cook for me? What sort of fellow was he?"

I lean back in my chair and gaze into the little cloud of smoke above my head. Though we spent but a few hours together, one doesn't quickly forget someone with whom one faces death.

"I judged him to be mid-fifties or so, average height, maybe 170 pounds. He wore a full yet well-trimmed beard, going gray. He spoke with authority, but without bravado. He said he had been licensed by Trinity House for twenty-five years. I suspect he was one of the best pilots hereabout. He may have thought to board the *Lawson* as there are often large awards made to pilots who save a vessel in distress."

"I would think it would have to be a rather large sum to overcome the sense of impending danger," Dagenham observes. I choose to avoid further speculation into Cook's mental state and continue my account.

Courtesy of the Gibson Family Collection
William (Billy Cook) Hicks

It was very dark by now. In response to their request, we put a ladder over the side and Cook climbed up with some difficulty. The seas were too rough for the lifeboat to lay beside, so we dropped a line, and they set themselves a good distance off our stern. After Cook's formal request to come aboard was made and granted, I introduced Bent Libby and myself and invited the pilot to my cabin.

"He was dressed in oilskins and sodden leather boots. The poor fellow looked half-frozen. As we walked aft, he looked aghast at the condition of my ship. Nearly all structures—hatches, vents, and wheelhouse—were dented, crushed, or mangled. Lines and tattered sails lay about the deck. Before we reached my salon, another lifeboat arrived on our starboard quarter.

"'It's the *Henry Dundas*,' Cook explained. 'She's out of St. Mary's, our largest island, due east of here.'

"Their coxswain hailed us and offered assistance. I called back that we had anchors set and would stay the night. With luck we would move off in the morning. His reply was the same as that of the *Charles Deere James*: We were in a dangerous location, and they offered to take off our crew. Jesus, I thought, how many lifeboats must I argue with tonight? Anyway, I declined, but queried Cook, 'Sir, is there a steam tug within these isles?'

"'There are two tugs and a steamer, but these are based at Falmouth, on the mainland. They would be eight or more hours from here in this weather, if they would care to venture it.'

"While we were discussing such assistance, the *Henry Dundas* gave up attempting to maintain a position on our starboard quarter. They moved off so as to encircle us while we considered our options. But as they rounded our stern, a cross wave caught them broadside and pushed them under our overhang. Riding up against us, they snapped their mizzenmast. Lines and canvas fell upon their crew. These impacts were repeated several times before they were able to push themselves away from the *Lawson* and into open waters.

"Cook, Libby, and I rushed to the rails, concerned for the seaworthiness of the lifeboat and the well-being of her crew. As they passed beside us again, they called up, 'We're returning to St. Mary's. … We are badly damaged. Will you not send your crew back with us?'

"Again, I refused. But I requested they radio Falmouth for tugs to come most urgently. They agreed, but asked, 'Billy, will you come in with us?' I looked at Cook as he shook his head no. 'Have you any messages for us?' Again, he indicated no. With that the *Henry Dundas* moved off, bailing desperately to avoid being swamped by the following seas."

Dagenham scribbles furiously to capture these details. I pause now to allow him time to catch up. He looks at me and smiles. "Thank you, Captain. I'm afraid I'm getting a bit of writer's cramp." He flexes his fingers rapidly. I'm glad it's him doing all this writing and not me. After another minute, he signals that I should resume.

"It was about seven o'clock when we arrived at my salon. The wind had slackened slightly, though the gusts were still thirty knots or so, coming from the west-northwest. Once his oilskins were doffed, I asked Billy Cook, 'Will you take some hot coffee?' I handed him a delicate blue and white cup from the *T. W. Lawson* service collection. He accepted it gratefully in his reddened hands. By the look on his face, I think he was taken aback by the luxury of my quarters. While he sipped, I recapped our situation.

"'Mr. Cook, we are twenty-five days out of Philadelphia. As you can see from our condition, we have been through a brutal crossing. My men are exhausted, and we have but few sails left.'

"I directed him to a large chart lying on the table. 'Will you confirm our exact position and suggest a path of departure once this storm passes by?'

"He placed his cup down and traced with his finger across my chart. 'Sir, you are here, between Nundeep and Gunners, about two miles to the west of Annet Island. This position is most treacherous. I suggest that you make way tonight, as you are nearly surrounded by rocks and ledges. The tide now ebbs away to the west.'

"With the gravest expression I could muster, I told him, 'Out of the question. My crew and ship are incapable of such a maneuver. The *Lawson* wears poorly in the best of conditions. Without adequate sails, without open waters, without a more experienced crew—tacking would be impossible. Our anchors, five tons each, are well set. Surely a tug will arrive by morning!'

"'I mean no disrespect, Captain,' he said. 'But your anchors will not hold against these seas. The seabed here is covered with rocks and seaweed. When the tide turns again, the waves will be relentless. I came aboard to pilot you to safety. Of course, it is your decision, but I recommend you take the risk and get underway immediately.'

"For the last time, I insist, 'I will not attempt to get underway in these conditions!'"

"Sounds like neither option was any good, Captain," Dagenham observes.

"Ah, isn't hindsight clear as rainwater?... I walked out on him, left him with Libby. He had my decision. I felt, perhaps, if Bent could talk to him he'd see we had no choice but to ride it out. I guess he must have requested coffee and biscuits for the crew of the *Charles Deere James*. I saw the steward bring a canteen and pouch to the deck."

"Captain, what of the *Charles Deere James*? They were tethered to the *Lawson*, no?"

"That's right." Dagenham is relentless in his examination. Frankly, I am growing weary of the subject, and, as we approach the climactic hours of that ill-begotten night, I am only reluctantly compliant.

"The first lifeboat had remained for what—nearly three hours— in frigid, dirty weather. The coffee and biscuits could only have been small comfort to a cold, wet crew. They hailed us just before eight o'clock.

"'Hello, the *Lawson*!... We've a man injured.'

"Billy came to the rail and called back, 'What's the matter? ... Who's injured?'

"'It's William Francis. He's gone unconscious,... Acts like a dead man. Could be a wave knocked him against the side....

Maybe he's suffering from exposure.... We must go in or he will be truly dead.... Will you come with us, Billy?'

"'No.... If you come alongside ... you'll get smashed like the *Henry Dundas.*'

"'Come down the warp then.... Once we leave, we'll not be back tonight,' called the coxswain.

"Cook turned to me, a pleading look in his eyes. 'They've got to go in. Captain. For the last time, save yourself and your crew! Abandon this ship, for she is surely doomed.'

"What could I say that I hadn't said already? I would not abandon my ship. I was confident that my anchors would hold. I replied, 'Mr. Cook, you may stay or go—that's up to you.'

"He bowed his head and nodded slowly. Neither of us spoke another word. He walked back to the rail and shouted down to his crew, 'Take William Francis ashore. ... I will stay the night here. ... Keep a watch on our riding lights. ... If necessary, we'll send up flares to request a lifeboat. ... Safe home now!'

"They loosed the warp and moved off to the east. Cook stood at the rail and watched till they had disappeared into the darkness. I wonder now, what must he have been thinking. Beyond the rocks and Annet Island, the faint lights of St. Agnes were barely visible. He remained on deck a long time.

"I asked Bent to stay with the pilot and I returned to my stateroom. 'Bring him to me when he's ready to come,' I told him. Meanwhile, I checked with Crocker. I wanted to know how things stood in the fo'csle, the wheelhouse, and the engine room. The poor fellow arrived bleary-eyed, wearing the stubble of weeks since his last shave.

"'We're beat to hell,' he reported, 'but still riding well enough. The men are very quiet, so you know they're nervous. Even the complainers have retreated to their bunks. They lie and listen to crashing waves and howling winds. Occasionally, we all jump at a windblown door banging shut like a thunderclap.'

"I nodded and requested further reports on the half-hour."

"You were fully confident in your decision to stay?" Dagenham asks.

I look at him with reproach pouring from my eyes. "Don't be tedious, Francis! My first duty as a master is the safety of my crew. Ship and cargo come second, always! Of course, I was confident. My God, man! I had 250 tons of chain out, each link weighing eighty pounds. Two five-ton anchors were properly deployed. I simply could not believe they would not hold!"

The reporter rocks back in his chair. "I didn't mean to suggest … but it's a question that our readers will be asking …"

His voice trails off into a moment of painful silence. When I finally resume, it's to Dagenham's visible relief.

"When Cook came in with Libby, I asked the steward to bring more coffee. At first, things were quiet and a bit awkward. To ease the tension, I asked Cook about his family.

"'Elizabeth and I have nine children,' Cook replied. 'One of my boys is on the *Charles Deere James*. And you?'

"'Wife, Jennie, and two sons—Orville and Richard.'

"This subject quickly exhausted, I struggled to find additional conversation. "Tell me, Mr. Cook, have you seen many wrecks in these waters?'

"'I've seen a few,' he replied. I can still see him run a hand through his wet, graying hair as he reflected further on my question.… 'Just last year, we had two—the *Magdeleine* and the

54

King Cadwallon. But there have been hundreds here, over the years.'

"'Let's hope that tug gets here by morning,' I replied.

"'Let's hope we are here by morning, Captain.'

"I remember being taken aback by this last remark, but making no response. We could only wait now to see which of us had made the better prediction of our fate. About ten o'clock the ship began to drag noticeably. The tide was turning and the waves building higher. Force-eight winds pushed them and us toward Annet. Libby and I looked at each other and then at Cook. I jumped up and paced. I offered pipe tobacco and we smoked. The requested reports from Crocker were increasingly ominous. When our lights flickered, Libby left to visit Rowe in the engine room. Once again, we settled back into those leather chairs and closed our eyes, trying, or pretending, to sleep. Then, bang! We heard a huge report, like a cannon shot. Bent returned in dripping oilskins, a vacant look in his eye.

"'Port anchor chain, Captain. She's parted. The starboard anchor can't hold us alone. I've told the crew to don life jackets, but most didn't need to be told. We should do the same.'

"I looked at him wide-eyed, still trying to accept the evidence of my ears. I went to the telephone and rang Crocker in the fo'csle. 'Mr. Crocker,' I shouted, 'we'll shortly be on the rocks! Assemble the men.... Get them on deck.... When the starboard chain goes ... there won't be much time! God be with you all.'

"Libby presented life jackets to Cook and me. As we fitted them to our bodies, the starboard chain parted, again with a terrific noise. The lights flickered again. I turned to Cook and said, 'Sir, you were right and I was wrong. I have done you a great disservice by allowing you to stay aboard.'

"Before the pilot could respond, Libby stepped between us. 'No time for that! Get into the rigging! Let's go, now!'

"We ran out on deck, into a darkness unrelieved by our riding lights. Squalling rain blew into our faces, nearly blinding us. We squinted to make out the dark forms running hither and yon, but could make no recognition. My God, what a howling mess! I never saw Cook again. Bent had my arm and led me to the spanker—the seventh mast. He gave me a push as I found the ratlines. I began to climb. 'Good luck,' I heard him shout against the wind. Then he disappeared. Oh, Jesus!"

I pause and take a few deep breaths. I can feel myself breaking into a sweat. I can't move past this scene. Bent was always like that, looking out for the other fellow. After a moment, I think to pull on my pipe, but it has gone out.

"I was about forty or fifty feet above the deck when the ship hit. She rolled progressively over onto her starboard beam. The sound of steel grinding against granite was eerie, like the trumpeting of a charging elephant, I imagine. The ripping hull gave out metallic reports, as steel plates parted from underlying skeletal beams. No. 7 mast, seventeen tons of once impressive solidity, now wavered, snapping the three tons of wire rigging that once held it erect."

Photo by author
The treacherous shoals near Shag Rock

Dagenham, silent and transfixed, has stopped writing. He stares at me, mouth agape.

I ignore his reaction and plough on. "Some cried out. I could hear their screams carried aft upon the wind. For some reason, I was not prompted to do so. Not out of bravery, mind you. I just was consumed by the physical effort of clinging to the ratlines, entwining my arms and legs against the sharp jolts each wave produced as we were tossed against a rock formation west of Annet. I'm told they call it Shag Rock."

"What thoughts went through your mind, Captain, as what seemed, I'm sure, like certain death approached?"

Dagenham waits for my response. I don't share everything with him, but I do make one more admission.

"I prayed!… I'm not what you'd call a pious fellow. But I am a believing Christian. It is hard to be the regular churchgoing sort when you spend nine or ten months a year at sea. I remember my father used to read the Psalms to his crew on a Sunday. I never did. But that night, I recited the verses I could remember."

"And then?"

"I was only aloft that mast twenty minutes or so, but it seemed like an hour. As the rolling of the ship progressed, the few masts that hadn't crumpled and fallen were nearly horizontal. At this point, I was only twenty or thirty feet over the pounding surf. I heard the No. 6 groaning and it began to fall. I released myself from the rigging and dropped, feet first, into the maelstrom below."

"What do you recall of your time in the water?" the reporter asks.

"The shock of the icy cold water is first and foremost. The weight of falling rigging pushed me under. It must have been then that my ribs broke, because I can remember having the wind knocked out of me and being unable to refill my lungs. A pain was shooting through my chest like a red-hot poker. I attempted to push myself away from the rocky ledge and float myself clear of the stern section, which had parted from rest of the ship. Once I was outside the shelter of the stern remnant, the waves pounded me against the rocks. That's when I broke my wrist, trying to protect myself from being dashed against the ledge."

Dagenham returns to note taking. "Were you conscious all the time? Could you swim?"

"I must have retained some degree of consciousness because, otherwise, I believe I should have drowned. But it was not a state of alertness or clear thinking. I was aware of pain and the frigid cold invading my body. Because of my wrist, I could not swim. But I did kick my legs as long as I was able. The life jacket was my salvation. I really don't remember washing up at Hellweathers or being pulled out of the water by Mr. Rowe."

I sit back, exhausted by the emotions triggered in the telling. My companion scribbles furiously and without further comment.

The front door suddenly opens. Israel pops his head in to say, "The ferry, Mr. Dagenham. It's rounding Gugh Island just now. You must hurry not to miss her."

The journalist stuffs his papers into his valise and rushes to the door. "Thank you, Captain. Sorry to have to hurry so. I'll be back once more." With that he heads off down the hill to the quay. As I watch him running down the path, I spot his valise, flapping against his side. Damn! I forgot to nick him for my drink!

Photo by author

Hellweathers Carn
where Rowe and Dow were rescued

Chapter Six

Israel steps inside again. He is home somewhat early from his day of sailmaking. I greet him and return to my seat in the now-dim parlor.

"Good afternoon, Mr. Dow."

I notice that he always neglects to refer to me as Captain Dow, but I am past being annoyed by it. "I'm glad to see you, Mr. Hicks." I pause, not sure whether to open up with him.... Oh, what the hell!

"I want to express again how grateful I am for the care and hospitality you and Charlotte are providing to Mr. Rowe and me. Though you've never asked, I'm confident my company will be generous in covering your outlays."

I suspect Israel is embarrassed at my raising this delicate issue, because he casts his eyes away from me. "Yes, ... well, ... that's fine. I guess the wife will be landing soon. I better get a few lights lit and stoke the fire."

He doffs his overclothes and lights a lamp. "Oh, I meant to mention, I have heard from Mr. Kirkpatrick, our Collector of Customs. He says there is to be a ceremony to honor the crew of the *Slippen*."

I am momentarily perplexed. Then, I deduce the *Slippen* must be the vessel that brought Rowe and me to safety. "Richly deserved! When shall this take place?"

"He isn't quite sure. Your government man, Mr. Hooper, told Kirkpatrick that medals will be given to each member of crew by the United States government. So it's whenever these can arrive from America, I suppose. I trust that you will still be here at the time?"

"I would like that very much. I would also like to meet and thank your man.... I think his name is Freddie Hicks. I understand he was most heroic in retrieving me from Hellweathers Carn. Would it be possible to have him stop by at his convenience? I'd go to him, for sure, were I less fragile."

Israel drops into his accustomed chair and removes his boots. "You mean Freddie Cook. I'll mention it to him. He has been a bit withdrawn since the loss of his father."

"Sorry, how is that? I thought he was a Hicks."

Israel raises his eyes to heaven, understanding my dilemma. "Ah, his proper name is Freddie Hicks. I guess there's so many of the Hicks family hereabout that we sometimes use another family name to keep ourselves straight. Pilot Billy and his family are known by the name of Cook."

I nod knowingly, though it seems rather confusing to me. He goes on to explain that a gig, rather than a full-sized lifeboat, was used the morning after the sinking, being easier to maneuver among the ledges and outcroppings of rock near the *Lawson's* final position. In that craft, besides himself, were Obadiah Hicks, Osbert Hicks and his son Fred, Freddie Cook, Grenfell Legg—a coastguardsman, William Treneary, and George Mortimer.

Courtesy of the Gibson Family Collection
The crew of the Slippen — Israel Hicks (far left),
Freddie Cook Hicks (fourth from the left)

"This doesn't include," he added, "the others who came out to your ship the previous evening: Abraham Hicks, William Francis Hicks, James Hicks, Albert Hicks, Stephen Hicks, Jack Hicks, and Walter Long. So, you see, it's easy to get your Hickses mixed up."

I shake my head in amazement. "Well, anyway, this fellow Freddie Cook saved my life. Though I was in such a state on the day, I can tell you nothing of what transpired."

Israel's eyes squint a bit. He pulls and strokes his mustache in silence. "It was a somber morning.... We set out around seven, suspecting what had happened to the *Lawson*, as the smell of kerosene was thick in the air. The waves were still quite wild, and we rowed with difficulty against them. We eventually discovered the ship's remains, turned turtle and floating half-submerged off Annet Island. We approached the island, noticing that mangled bodies and limbs had washed ashore. We landed, looking for survivors. That's when we found your Mr. Allen, huddled beside a rock, desperately broken, in terrible pain. His ribs, smashed upon the rocks, must have punctured his lungs. We took him back to St. Agnes promptly, but he was dead within a matter of hours."

Courtesy of the Gibson Family Collection
Fore section of the Lawson
December 14, 1907

I run my hands down the back of my neck, tensed by this account and by the recollection that Allen was among the best of my crew. Poor bastard must have suffered terribly.

Israel resumes, "We went back out, but by two-thirty or so, we'd found no one else alive. Deciding to return to St. Agnes, we rowed past Hellweathers Carn. It was then that I spotted two figures wedged into a crevice—you and Mr. Rowe. As Rowe was the able one, we threw him a rope. After several tries we succeeded, and he tied it about his waist and pushed himself off into the icy waters. He screamed in pain as we pulled him to us. We took him back to St. Agnes, and Fred Hicks and I carried him here to the house. That's when my part ended."

"Oh? How was that?"

"The crew was anxious to return for you. Isaac Legg and Albert Hicks took our places and the *Slippen* shoved off shortly after Rowe was landed. Several of the crew told me what happened, though. They got back to Hellweathers about four in the afternoon. As you were fully disabled, they knew a different approach was required. They beached the *Slippen* on a ledge near the Carn. Freddie Cook, taking rope, oilskins, and a life ring, got out. He fastened one end of the rope to a large rock and tied the other end around his waist. Then he slipped over the edge and into the churning surf. He swam about forty yards to where you were lying. He wrapped you in the oilskins and tied the rope around you. As the crew pulled the rope, Freddie swam, holding your head above water with the aid of the ring. Once landed on the ledge, he carried you across a distance of slippery rocks and back to the *Slippen*. All this he did whilst mourning his father."

"Such bravery!... I am overwhelmed."

"His courage was no greater than that of Billy Cook," Israel replies tersely. "Getting aboard your ship and declining to leave—that, too, was bravery. And he paid for it with his life."

I don't know how to respond. There is a moment of awkward silence, broken only when Charlotte makes her entrance, having returned from St. Mary's with her grocery items. We rise, and Israel goes to help her with her burden. I wander off to visit Rowe, something I am trying to do daily. But finding him in the midst of a nap, I decide not to disturb him. I return to my room to await supper. I try to read a book Mr. Hicks has loaned me, *The Spoilers*. It's about the gold rush to the Klondike. I am enjoying it; but now I can't concentrate. I decide to get some air. I venture into the garden behind the Hicks's house. The late afternoon is rather cool, and it is getting dark. Damn! Stupid of me not to wear the coat

I have on loan. After a few minutes of gazing out at the shifting gray mass that is Broad Sound, I am cold and must go in.

Eventually, the evening meal is called. Charlotte leads the conversation—typical chatter of encounters in Hughtown, her visit with the children, and who was aboard the ferry. "Did you have an enjoyable visit with that newspaper man, Captain?" Charlotte inquires.

"Very nice, ma'am. I expect he may call again tomorrow, if the weather is fair." I return to my fish stew.

Israel makes a poor show of interest and I don't blame him. Perhaps he also feels the weight of our prior discussion. I cannot help but resent his insinuations that I am responsible for the death of his pilot, Billy Cook. I know he also holds me responsible for the loss of my ship and crew. Doesn't he realize that we were helpless before a storm of that magnitude? I wonder what he would have had me do, without the sails to maneuver. How would he have suggested wearing the *Lawson* before rocks and ledges in the midst of a hurricane? When the eating is finished, I excuse myself and retire.

Chapter Seven

I try to read again but give it up. My mind flies here and there, avoiding the issues that roil within. I snuff the lamp and hope that sleep will quiet my mind. Surprisingly, I am able to fall off without much delay. But my brain continues to slip its tether. In a dream, I am carried away in time and place. I am once again the twenty-eight-year-old master of the schooner *Stampede*. We have just taken on a shipment of lumber at Mobile, with Port au Prince as our destination. Besides filling the hold, we have a deck load to carry, and *Stampede* is riding very low in the water.

I notice Mr. Moon, my first mate. He, too, is from Hancock County. He is upset with me over something. What was it?... Oh, right! The log! We have no chip log, the device used to track the speed made by our vessel. I had ordered a new patent log before leaving Boston. The old one had been lost, and I neglected to check for the replacement prior to our departure.

"Not to worry," I tell him. "I've sailed this vessel enough to be a reasonable judge of her speed. I will give you figures each day to record in the log book, and we will make corrections with the sextant."

I know I should have remedied our lack in the port of Mobile, but I am comforted that there is a brand-new log awaiting us in Boston. And after all, we had no problem on the voyage to Mobile. The weather had been fair, and sightings of the sun were easily had each day.

But now, two days out of Mobile, a gale has formed and the skies are heavily shrouded. I order sails close reefed—first the main, then the fore, and finally the jib. This turns into an all-night effort as the jib blows out before it can be furled. Setting out a replacement in these high winds is wicked.

Dimly, I can make out a vision of our decks, constantly awash. I call Moon aft and tell him, "Best start to pump—we may be taking on water." He returns after having put men to the task.

"The sounding rod shows over three feet of water in the well, Captain. I have both pumps attended and will rotate hands at regular intervals."

I nod and ask for regular reports of progress. After several hours, we work our way through it. One man continues to pump to keep up with what is apparently a leak. When all hands are required on deck, as when we make sail or reef, the leak goes unattended. Subsequently, both pumps must be employed to recover the loss and suck her out....

I toss around in this troubled dream, recalling the head winds we must fight as we work our way up the Gulf Stream. Then, gratefully, we catch an easterly wind. This will take us on a line from which we may work back southwest toward Haiti. There are successive squalls throughout our days. A week passes without taking the sun and fixing our latitude. Eventually, the seas moderate a bit—

I awaken with a start. My bedclothes are damp with sweat. I kick them off. There is no moonlight tonight, so I must fumble in the dark for a drink of water. Within minutes I must doze off, because my former dream recurs....

Mr. Moon approaches the poop deck with his typically grave expression.

"Captain," he chides, "it's been seven days without a sighting or a log reading. We may soon find ourselves running aground or worse."

I shrug my shoulders and concede his point. "I agree. If the weather doesn't clear by the end of the first dogwatch, we'll heave to. I would not be surprised if we should be near land."

The end of the watch comes and it is still raining. I order the flying jib furled and bring *Stampede* into the wind. One of the crew is placed on lookout; another mans the pump. The barometer is rising, and I am hopeful the skies will clear by midnight.

Later, I visit my cabin to collect my pipe. I stand with my feet wide apart to answer the heavy rolling of the vessel. My door is open as Moon and Mr. Berry, the cook, come by. I share a story with them—previous days on the Spanish Main. But, in mid-sentence, I am interrupted by the call of the lookout.

"Breakers! Breakers! All hands on deck!"

I drop my pipe and dash up the companionway. "Wear ship," I exclaim to the man at the wheel.

I can hear the roar of the surf breaking upon a reef. If we can't escape being tossed upon the coral, it will rip *Stampede*'s hull like the seat of a fat man's trousers. I look forward and see a wall of ocean coming toward us.

"Hold on the main peak, and every man look out for that sea!"

The bow of *Stampede* rises until, I swear, she's standing upon her stern. Then she tips and the jib boom is plunged into the depths. All of us on deck are right behind, clutching to the rigging for dear life as the seas engulf us. To our relief, up she rises. Twice more rollers hit us, but on the lee bow. And these, acting upon the rudder, make the schooner turn. She files away on a starboard tack.

As we gain steerage way, I order soundings with the deep-sea lead. When men are ready at the fore chains, I luff the schooner into the wind so as to arrest our headway. The lead is heaved. It then takes three men to haul it home.

"Twelve fathoms," Mr. Moon reports. I turn *Stampede* hard alee and drive her as fast as she will go. Another sounding is taken after twenty minutes, and we cannot find bottom within thirty fathoms. We have escaped!

I see Moon looking at me sternly. Perhaps he is right to do. I have risked my vessel, cargo, and crew, all for the cost of a log!

Chapter Eight

My God, what a dream! It has left me uneasy. The new day is overcast, and a strong wind brings a wet chill that seems to penetrate my bones. I huddle close to the fireplace, but as the Hickses expend their coal with caution, the fire burns low and without much warmth. I'll wager that Dagenham will not come today—not till the weather improves.

Charlotte has cleared away the breakfast and is attending to Rowe. I wonder how much longer I must impose upon the hospitality of this house. My body is still a lump of aches and pains, and my wrist itches beneath its splint and wrappings.

I still await correspondence from Coastwise regarding arrangements for my return home. I assume I can find something headed for America in the port of Southampton. But I need money for clothing and personal items, as was promised in John Crowley's telegram two weeks ago.

Today is Sunday, and we have a special occasion. Rowe is joining us at table for dinner. His shattered knees still won't support his weight, but Israel has devised a means of mobility—a wheelbarrow. With settee cushions in its bed, Rowe is precariously seated atop, hands braced on either side, his useless legs draped over the front. He reminds me of a Siamese potentate being ferried about in a sedan chair. Israel's barrow, more accustomed to loads of sailcloth, nets, and anchor line, is navigated ably by our host from the rear of the house, through the parlor, and into the kitchen. The engineer seems to be immensely delighted to be freed from his incarceration and warmly received at table.

But he is not at all the confident thirty-five-year-old I met just five months ago in New York. Then, tousled locks of light brown hair topped his high forehead. His straight nose and strong chin framed a nearly ever-present smile. Now his matted hair seems dull, his smile tentative and fleeting. Israel carefully lifts him to a chair beside me.

"Welcome aboard, mate," I murmur to him as he settles in. He pats my arm in reply. Charlotte has gone full out for the occasion, with roast of beef, boiled potatoes, and canned peas. The celebration lacks only a ration of spirits for the crew.

After Israel intones a blessing, Charlotte dabs at her eyes and then begins serving up the steaming plates of food.

"Oh, isn't this nice, Mr. Rowe? It must have been so lonely, taking all your meals in solitude these many days."

Rowe seems to me at once embarrassed and overwhelmed. He manages a "Yes, ma'am" and fights off his tears.

"Mr. Hicks," I inquire, "have you had the opportunity to speak with Freddie Cook? I am still anxious to have a visit and properly thank him for his brave efforts on our behalf."

Israel gazes blankly into his cup of dark, strongly brewed tea, the favored household drink. His brow furrows; he clears his throat. "I'm afraid I haven't, Mr. Dow. Not yet. But I'll make a point of it tomorrow for certain."

He never looks me in the eye during this discourse, and the tension between us continues. As usual, Charlotte takes up the slack in the table conversation with items of current interest in the small St. Agnes community or with queries to Rowe and myself about our lives back in America. Our country is always referred to as such, never as "the United States."

After the meal, I follow Israel as he wheels Rowe back to his room. It's not that I can offer any assistance, as my wrist is still braced and wrapped. But I hope to linger for some conversation in the lull of midafternoon.

When Rowe is properly ensconced on his bed and Israel has departed with his makeshift wheelchair, I broach the subject so assiduously avoided between us. After a bit of stammering, I begin.

"Mr. Rowe, we haven't spoken this last four weeks of the night the *Lawson* went down, nor of the efforts expended by yourself for our survival. Till now, I was reluctant to bring it up, for reasons you might well imagine. I suspect you may have had similar feelings. But now, I'd like your account, if you're willing to share it. Once we are finally quit of this place, we may not have such an opportunity again."

Rowe toys with the wrapper of his lost B-L chewing tobacco, sodden and discolored from the seawaters that invaded his pocket that awful night. It has become for him a talisman of sorts. He turns his now-sad eyes toward me.

"I did wonder about your silence, Captain. It's hard to shake off troublesome memories, isn't it? Perhaps talking about it now will allow us to put these thoughts away."

I agree and wait patiently. He tosses the wrapper onto the bed.

"Oh, Jesus! Where shall I begin? I ... Well, ... Late that night, Mr. Libby called me up from the engine room. I was reporting upon conditions when the first anchor chain snapped. When the order came to get to the rigging, I unlaced my shoes and cut myself a length of signal halyard, which I looped around my body several times. Then I mounted beside the spanker."

"That's where I took refuge. Of course, in the dark and the driving rain, it's no wonder we didn't see each other."

Rowe chews his cheek briefly, then resumes. "I climbed the ratlines to the sheer pole. When the rigging began to fall, I landed back on deck. Then the big wave struck her and her sticks toppled. It was every man for himself. We were all in the water. For a moment I was tangled in the rigging, but eventually I managed to wriggle free. Then, by God's hand, up pops a length of twelve-by-twelve with a good-sized iron spike stuck into it. It must have been a beam from the centerline bulkhead. I grabbed hold of the spike, as I cannot swim a stroke. Another sailor, might have been the fireman Olanssen, bobbed up and clung to the other end of the beam. But when the seas lifted up his end, his hold failed and he was tossed off.… I never saw him again."

Rowe draws a deep breath and places his hands over his eyes. He is on the brink of a good cry, and I may not be far behind. I rise and go look out the window to give him some privacy. He blows his nose and eventually composes himself. When he has done so, I return to my chair and ask, "Were there any others that you saw after the ship turned over?"

His voice quavers. "Not after … I did see George Allen attempt to escape by walking out the bowsprit. He must have thought he might leap to the ledges below. But when the ship struck, he was tossed into the void."

"Yes, and with awful consequence. God rest his soul.…" Rowe goes silent till I prod, "What happened next?"

"I watched as the *Lawson* broke apart between masts No. 6 and 7. The fore section slid below while the stern floated off, held up by the huge tank inside. It was drifting closer and closer to a rocky crag with a high, ugly pinnacle. A huge wave raised the stern high above and sent it crashing upon this point, bursting the tank open like a ripe cantaloupe. That was the last I saw of her."

I draw my chair closer to Rowe's bed. "How did you come upon Hellweathers then?"

"I drifted about, to the lee of Annet, for several hours. As daylight was approaching, I felt my feet touch bottom. Looking around me, I could see a reef extending off in the direction of the lighthouse. The tide was ebbing and I pushed my timber along the reef, looking for a safe landing point. I was deathly cold and shivering constantly. As I approached a high point of the Carn, I released my grip on that iron spike. My palm is still bruised and scarred from the hours of clinging for dear life."

He extends his open hand so that I might examine the marks of his struggle. The darkened, shredded skin repulses me, and I am ashamed of my reaction. I look away.

"I pushed off and kicked mightily to gain a grasp on a high crevice nearby. I pulled myself up and over, rolling into a sandy bed of mussels exposed by the receding tide. My broken kneecaps prevented me from standing. But after gaining my breath, I crawled to a higher point, above the lapping waves, and looked about for signs of a rescue party."

"Is that when you found me?"

"No, it was nearly two hours before I saw you drifting toward my position. You were in your life jacket and had wrapped your mackintosh around your broken arm. I crawled out to grab for you and pull you to safety."

"May I say now how grateful I am for your courageous effort? Every movement must have been terribly painful for you."

"Ah, you'd have done as much for me, Captain. We Maine boys stick together, don't we?"

I give what I hope is a benevolent smile. "Ayah. That we do. Please, go on."

"You and I lay there for hours, till maybe early afternoon. We couldn't speak really, just moaning over our injuries. Then I saw a small craft, a six-oared gig, passing nearby. I waved your mack and called out to them. Maneuvering with difficulty, they approached as close as they dared. One of the crew threw a rope to me and said, "Tie it around the captain and we'll pull him aboard.' But I refused, knowing that you had internal injuries—who knew how severe. I didn't think you'd survive being hauled about. Knowing you were in a safe place, I looped the rope under my arms and slid off into the water."

I laugh now and remark upon this apparent abandonment. But Rowe protests, "Nay, Captain! I explained to them how they might approach more easily from that mussel bed where I did first make landing. But they took me straight to St. Agnes, promising to return promptly."

"I have no memory at all of my own rescue. I only recall the shock of being back in those icy waters,... and the smell of kerosene all about."

Rowe lies back, seemingly wrung out by his story and the memories of cold and pain. "You know," he observes, "Israel, our Mr. Hicks, claims he was the first to catch sight of me that day. Sure, he would have just as soon I was Billy Cook instead."

I sigh to myself at this unwelcome observation. "Understandable. Were they very close?"

"Aye, the pilot fella, he was Israel's best friend."

Chapter Nine

Sleep eluded me again last night. I finally dozed for an hour or so at dawn, just long enough to make me late coming to breakfast. The good news is that Israel has already left for his workshop, and I am spared his silence and rebuking glances. I expect Dagenham will come today as the weather is fine and it is no longer the Sabbath. I look forward to these visits. The man is pleasant enough. And when he doesn't come around, the day seems to drag on.

Charlotte pours my tea and brings toast and beans from the stove. Now, as a down-east Yankee, I defer to no man in my enjoyment of a good pot of baked beans. But it strikes my palate strange to be served such for breakfast. And these Brit beans are different—not bad, just different. I linger over my tea as Charlotte washes up the dishes.

"Charlotte, would you have time for a chat? I'd be interested in your views on a matter that preys upon my mind."

My kindly hostess turns and smiles that beatific smile, like she's been waiting for such an invitation. She wipes her hands dry. "Why, Captain, it would be my pleasure to discuss whatever is bothersome to you. Perhaps I can be of help in some small way."

She takes one of the cups she has just washed and dried, and fills it with the black dregs from the bottom of the pot. Then she joins me at table, happy to turn away from household duties for a while.

"You must know, Charlotte, how eternally grateful I am for the hospitality and care I've been shown by you and Israel this last month. Soon I'll be able to travel and make my return to Boston."

"Oh, Captain, we are quite aware of your gratitude. You mustn't dwell upon it. Rather, you must look forward to the day of reunion that approaches, with Jennie and your sons."

I stroke my too-long mustaches, perhaps a nervous gesture, an act of impatience. This chat will not be about reunion with Jennie, if I can help it.

"Actually, what's on my mind is a bit delicate. I wouldn't wish you to mistake my motives. You see, it's Israel I'd like to ask about."

The missus sits back and stares at me, blinking quizzically. "Israel?"

"Yes, ma'am. You see, I learned only yesterday from Mr. Rowe that the lost pilot, Billy Cook, was Israel's closest friend."

She nods silently and takes a sip of her tea. The bitter leavings of the pot cause her to wince. "Why yes, Billy and Israel are … were like brothers."

"Charlotte, I sometimes get the feeling that Israel blames me for the loss of his friend, as surely as if I had wrung his neck."

"Oh, Captain, I'm sure that isn't so.… Israel isn't a great talker, even to myself. But I have learned over the years to read my husband. No, if he blamed you I would know it. He might well have refused you the hospitality of this house if he believed what you suggest."

"I'm pleased to hear you say so, ma'am. But it has been my experience that a man's brain often wrestles with his heart. This is what I have done these many days on St. Agnes. My head says one thing, but my heart ain't quite convinced. Could it be that your husband has the same wrestling match going on inside of him?"

Charlotte's chin begins to quiver, and her gaze avoids my own. She sets her tea down and stands abruptly. "I have told you what I believe to be true, Captain. What contradictions may affect your own mind, I cannot debate with you. But, as for Israel, I think there are none for you to worry about.... Will you excuse me?"

With that, she retreats from the room.... Guess I fouled my lines this time. And yet, what should I conclude? Is she sincere? Does she even know whereof she speaks? At the end of the day— as these Brits always say—what real difference should it make to me? Israel may hate my guts, but soon I'll be gone and it will not matter.

At dinner, Israel returns with news. In a low, matter-of-fact tone, he advises me, "I spoke to Freddie Cook this morning, Mr. Dow."

There! See how he again withholds the honorific, Captain! I'm convinced my suspicions are well founded.

"He's pleased that you wish to see him and has promised to stop in tonight after supper."

"Thank you for your assistance, Mr. Hicks. I look forward to it."

Israel nods and attends his plate. No further conversation between us ensues, though he chats with Rowe, who is again with us at table. I don't join in their conversation; I now keep my sails furled in Israel's presence. I would like to clear the air with the man, but I hesitate, not wanting to further alienate him while I'm a guest in his home.

After dinner, Dagenham makes his appearance. He offers a greeting to Israel as he comes in. They fall into a discussion regarding the planned ceremony of appreciation for the crew of the *Slippen*. Dagenham announces that he will request that the *Times* dispatch a photographer on the day. Now Israel returns to his sailmaking, leaving Dagenham and me to our business.

"Captain. I'm sorry to arrive so late, but there were a few other contacts I wished to make here on St. Agnes this morning as I'll be returning to London tomorrow."

I wonder who these other contacts might be but refrain from asking.

"I shall miss our chats, Francis."

This day is sunny and unseasonably mild. Also, the ocean is calm, so I'm sure Francis was pleased with that. As I'm feeling more limber this afternoon, I ask him, "Shall we take a stroll? It's an uncommonly nice day and walking no longer pains me quite so bad."

"A splendid suggestion. Let's do. But I'll need to bring my notes." He lifts his valise. "Shall we walk over to the churchyard?"

I agree and go off briefly to retrieve the coat and hat that have been loaned to me. When Francis and I move away from the house, I look down the hill to the quay, now empty and awaiting the afternoon ferry. To the east, Gugh Island is visible, connected to St. Agnes by a spit of white sand laid bare in the low tide.

"This is surely a beautiful place. Too bad days like today are so hard come by."

"My sentiments precisely, Captain."

We turn from the grassy footpath onto Old Lane, a lightly traveled, narrow thoroughfare. We follow it through Lower Town, where St. Agnes Church lies, not far below the seventeenth-century lighthouse. It is a short walk, but given my condition, we take it slow and easy. Dagenham, ever focused on his assignment, returns to the interrupted interview of three days ago.

"Our last conversation left you floating in waters off Annet Island, Captain. What further memories do you have of that time and the aftermath?"

"As I mentioned previously, Francis, I don't have clear memories at all. Rather, I have impressions of being wet, cold, and in pain. I don't even recall being pulled up on Hellweathers Carn by Mr. Rowe, though he has now described it for me. And I wasn't fully conscious during my rescue by the crew of the *Slippen*, though Israel has relayed the tale secondhand. I am hoping to meet Freddie Cook tonight. He's the hero that brought me safely to the *Slippen*."

Courtesy of Mr. Tom Hall
St. Agnes boathouse and slipway,
St. Agnes Church (behind), lighthouse (upper left)

Dagenham nods his apparent awareness of similar accounts. "Perhaps then, Captain, we should step back and consider the meaning of all that has transpired. How has this traumatic incident left you?"

I stop walking and turn to face the journalist. I feel my ire rising, and I take a deep breath to regain a semblance of control. "Francis, how am I supposed to feel, having seventeen men lose their lives on my watch? How should I present myself to the Crowley brothers, who entrusted me with both vessel and cargo? Shall I don sackcloth and ashes? Shall I flail myself with the cat-o'-nine-tails? Will that bring anyone back? Perhaps that's what your readers will wish to hear about—the repentant captain!"

Dagenham goes a shade paler than usual and stammers a response. "Please, Captain! That's not what I was suggesting at all.... Our readers will naturally be anxious to learn what, if anything, you will take away from this incident. You tell me. I shan't presume anything—only what you are willing to disclose."

I resume our stroll and he moves to stay abreast. He graciously gives me a few moments to check my temper. We walk in silence till we reach the churchyard. The place is deserted on this Monday afternoon. Puffy white clouds scud across the blue sky, throwing intermittent shadows here and there. Within the enclosure of ancient, lichen-encrusted stone walls, we find a grassy expanse, stone markers, and monuments scattered before us. None of these is particularly grand or ornate. These tablets, inscribed with the identities of their clients, cluster beside and behind the simple stone-block church. The building is topped with a low, stubby bell tower and a slate roof. Further on, a patch of bare soil covers a wide area just in front of the weeds and brambles that mark the end of consecrated ground.

"This must be the mass grave," Dagenham offers. "As I understand it, the bodies and body fragments of the *Lawson* crew were interred together. Of course, some were never recovered."

I feel a slight shudder and approach the scarred earth with the reverence that one might assume upon entering a great cathedral. Dagenham follows discreetly, a few steps behind. When I reach the spot, I remove my hat and recall the faces of my crew. I see Bent Libby first and foremost. I feel myself choking up again. How will I face his widow?... Then there's the cabin boy, Mark Sampson.... Poor, broken George Allen and the pilot, Billy Cook, I recall with respect bordering on affection. The others, I didn't know them well. A few were satisfactory hands; many were not.... But they were my responsibility. I can see all their images in the glass of memory.

I speak to Dagenham without facing him. "I told you before that I am not a pious man, just a simple, believing Christian. I believe these men will receive their just deserts from their Maker.... as you and I will surely do. It's too late for me to render them any meaningful service...."

I stop and ponder a bit. Is there not something, ... some little gesture ...? Turning to my companion, I suggest, "There is one thing I'd like to do while we are here. Do you have the customary bottle in your valise?"

Dagenham looks rather scandalized at my question. He nods slowly in the affirmative.

"Will you permit me?" I ask, holding out my good hand.

He fumbles with his valise and eventually retrieves the nearly full bottle that was given a temporary reprieve last time we met. He hands me the bottle with evident misgivings. I take the bottle and retract the well-seated cork with my teeth. Not a genteel act, but one necessitated by my injured wrist.

Facing the freshly turned soil, I stand as straight as my injuries allow. I raise the whisky in salute. My voice quavers at first. "To the mates and hands of the *Thomas W. Lawson*. The forces of nature once again have proved themselves more powerful than man and machine."

As I continue, a degree of resolve steadies me. "It is my regret that this great loss is visited upon your wives and children, mothers and fathers, brothers and sisters.... But I will do what you would do, were you in my place. I will return home, hopefully to another command. If such is granted me, I will do my best, as I tried to do it for you.... God save you all."

Quickly I put the bottle to my lips and take a generous swig. Perhaps too generous; it burns my throat a bit as it goes down. I pause to recover. Then I hand the bottle to Dagenham and invite him. "To the crew?"

He gives me a smile and nod of approval. I knew there was something about this fellow I liked, that I trusted. He raises the bottle to the grave and repeats with feeling, "To the crew!"

Abashedly, I hand him the cork and turn away. We linger quietly within the church grounds, being healed in the warm sunshine of this fine day. Later, I query him about his life back in London, but I learn very little. He explains that, as a bachelor man, his journalism consumes his time and attention.

Later, as we walk back up through Lower Town, he comments, "That toast to your crew was spot on, Captain. It gave proper respect to your men, but you also answered my question from earlier. As you said, a man does his best—that's all that can be expected of him. Sinking into a bog of remorse and guilt, whether real or imagined, gives comfort to no one. I hope I understand you correctly, Captain."

Close enough, I'm thinking. "You're doing fine, Francis. Now let's not have you missing the ferry."

Setting a slow but steady pace, we return to the Hicks's home. Upon arrival, we pause at the gate. He extends his hand and, grasping my left firmly, makes his goodbye.

"I'll send you a copy of my article, Captain. I hope you'll be pleased. You've given me your time and your honesty. I'm more than grateful."

"Francis, it's been a pleasure making your acquaintance. But I don't really need to read your article. No offense, but I trust you'll tell the tale as best you can. It's all a man can do, eh? Goodbye, my friend, and smooth sailing."

He turns to head back down the hill. Suddenly, he stops. He runs the thirty-odd paces back to the gate. "I mustn't forget." Pulling from his valise the unfinished bottle, he hands it to me. "A farewell gift," he says softly. Then he is gone.

I enter the house quietly, discreetly hiding the whisky, and repair to my room. There I await supper and my encounter with Freddie Cook Hicks.

Chapter Ten

At supper, Israel is more talkative than usual. He enthusiastically describes for me various items recently recovered from the *Lawson* by divers and those scavenging Annet's shoreline.

"It must have been richly furnished," Charlotte observes. "There was even fine china and glassware recovered."

"The captain's salon and stateroom were embarrassingly splendid," I reply. "Not at all what is normally provided for the master of an American trading vessel. But Mr. Lawson, the ship's namesake, was used to living on a grand scale. He felt that his ship ought to offer no less."

Not long after supper, there is a knock at the door. I am seated in the parlor, and I wait for Israel to answer it. A powerfully built young man stands at the threshold carrying a kerosene lantern. He wears a flat cap rather than the nautical, billed cap favored by Israel and Billy Cook. His dark eyebrows and mustache compliment a handsome face, giving an expression that is subdued, but not unfriendly.

"Evening, Israel. Grand day, wasn't it?"

Israel welcomes his visitor and introduces us. "Mr. Dow, here's Freddie Cook."

David M. Quinn

I stand and smile, offering my good hand, which he accepts readily. He looks me up and down.

"Well, Captain, I trust your injuries are healing nicely?"

I babble something about the fine care I'm receiving. I am busily attempting to read what might be the frame of mind of my visitor. Will he share Israel's resentments? Finally, I muster a presence of mind.

"Mr. Cook, I believe I owe my present well-being largely to you. Israel has kindly shared with me the story of your brave efforts on the day. I'm grateful to you for my rescue."

Freddie casts his eyes about the room, seemingly uncomfortable being the object of praise. Charlotte emerges from the kitchen and gives him a hug. An awkward moment of silence ensues. Wise Charlotte takes her husband's elbow and says, "Will you help me with the dishes, dear? I'm sure these gentlemen will excuse us."

Looking somewhat perplexed, Israel allows himself to be steered out of the parlor. Freddie and I are left to devise a way forward.

"How's Mr. Rowe progressing?" he finally asks.

"I'm afraid his knees still have him landlocked in his room. But Israel wheels him to the dinner table each day and that has brightened his mood lately. Soon, he may be able to manage crutches.... Will you sit a while?"

Courtesy of the Gibson Family Collection
Freddie Cook Hicks

"Actually, Captain, I have a lantern outside. I thought we might stroll down to the boathouse. Our RNLI lifeboat is housed there, and I thought you might be interested. I can also show you the gig, *Slippen,* from which your rescue was made."

I breathe a sigh of relief. This suggestion will afford us even greater privacy for our discussion. I nod and reply, "I'll just get my hat and coat."

Once we move beyond the house, the sparse lights of Middle Town and Upper Town can be seen above us. Though January temperatures prevail, it is a clear, pleasant evening. A new moon cedes to the many stars a temporary prominence. The wind carries the sound of waves lapping at the rocky shore. We begin our descent, slowly retracing the path traveled earlier this day with Francis.

As we proceed, Freddie describes the storied history of the Royal National Lifeboat Institution in whose service the men of St. Agnes are frequently volunteered. We reach the bottom of the hill and a clapboard boathouse set well above the high-water mark. St. Agnes Church is just off to the left, and the lighthouse beams its warnings from the hillside above us.

Freddie enters a side door and lights additional lanterns. Soon a warm, yellow glow illuminates the interior. The lifeboat *Charles Deere James* rests on a carriage set upon rails that extend from within the boathouse, out the main doorway, and along a stone slipway that leads to the water's edge. A windlass and cable stand at the head of this track for drawing vessels from the water into this shelter. At one side of the boathouse, several gigs rest upside down on blocks of wood. These six-oared rowboats include the *Slippen*, which Freddie proudly exhibits for my benefit.

After a further few moments of looking around, I turn to Freddie. "I want to mention to you my deepest sympathy for the loss of your father...."

I see Freddie stiffen in reaction to my overture. I hurry to complete my statement before I lose this opportunity. "Though we met only briefly, and under trying circumstances, I am left with great respect for his courage and ability."

Freddie sniffs, clears his throat, and spits. I wait for this surge of emotion to pass.

He answers, "Father bet against the odds and lost. It wasn't the first time he had challenged the sea in pursuit of a rescue. And, he was used to winning his bets. I believe his head told him your ship was doomed, but his heart wouldn't let him sail away."

I look around for someplace to sit and rest myself. I select one of the wooden stools within the workshop. "You must know, if I could have maneuvered the *Lawson* as he requested, I would have done so. With hardly any canvas and rocky shoals at every turn...."

He interrupts me, "You needn't convince me of your good faith, Captain. I doubt that the *Lawson's* owners would entrust such a tremendous vessel to a mariner lacking experience and good judgment. Like my father, you found yourself without good options. I don't hold you responsible for his death."

I feel a weight and a tightness leave my body. "I'm relieved to learn so, Mr. Cook. I wish Israel shared your view. I believe he does not."

Freddie too pulls a stool from across the room and sits facing me. "Captain, you may find this a bit strange, but I don't think Israel really believes you caused my father's death, or the deaths of your crew. But he is laying the blame upon you."

"I'm sorry, I don't understand."

Freddie smiles. "He must blame you ... because, otherwise, he must blame himself."

"Blame himself?"

"Yes. You see, Israel came to view my father as an older brother. They grew up very close to each other and were mutually protective. Israel wasn't with us that night on the *Charles Deere James*. However misguided, he feels that, were he there, he could have prevailed upon my father not to go aboard the *Lawson*. He wouldn't admit it to you or to me. He might not be able to admit it to himself. You, unfortunately, are the most eligible candidate to carry his imagined guilt."

I am at a loss for words. I pull my burl pipe and fumble through my pockets for some tobacco.

"Best you not light up in here, Captain. Paints, varnish, lots of combustibles are stored in here. Shall we start back?"

I step outside, still befuddled by what I have just heard. Freddie extinguishes the lanterns within and latches the door. As we climb the hill, he changes the subject, anxious to lighten the mood of our discussion.

"The *Lawson* was one hell of a ship, Captain. When I saw her that night, it was hard to believe she was real."

"A hell of a ship? Yes. You don't know the half of it."

I answer a stream of questions he has about the schooner and its final voyage. After some minutes of this, he mercifully lets the subject drop.

I lose myself in silent thoughts about Israel, his true feelings, his unconscious recriminations. How is Freddie able to discern these when even Charlotte seems unaware? I am able to put these questions aside only temporarily as he leaves me at the Hicks's door.

"Thank you for your visit tonight," I conclude. "I appreciate what you have shared with me."

Freddie nods knowingly. "Goodnight, Captain, and safe journey back to America."

I watch his receding figure and the lantern's glow until they disappear over the edge of the hill.

Chapter Eleven

January 17th, 1908

The last few days have been uneventful, proceeding more slowly than I would prefer. With Dagenham gone, there hasn't been much to pique my interest. I'm still trying to plough through *The Spoilers*, but I find myself lost in a daydream after a few pages. Happily for me, this morning's ferry brought the long-awaited packet from John Crowley. When Israel brings it to the house, I carry it to my room and tear it open. A paper slip falls to the floor. It is a cashier's check drawn for seven hundred British pounds.

The accompanying letter reads:

> *Dear George,*
>
> *I hope this message finds you in restored health and ready to undertake the return home. I have been in touch with Jennie repeatedly, assuring her of your convalescence and describing arrangements for your return. She has asked me to convey her love and concern. Orville and Richard are also eager to have you home again.*
>
> *I have arranged passage for you on the American Line out of Southampton. The enclosed ticket*

will cover your passage to New York on the SS Philadelphia, departing the twenty-fifth of this month. The cashier's check should be sufficient to cover transit to Southampton and rail passage from New York to Boston. You are further authorized to offer an appropriate compensation to the St. Agnes family providing lodging and board to you and Edward Rowe. It is my understanding that Rowe's return must await further healing.

Once you have confirmed this schedule of return, please advise by telegram. I am looking forward to personally welcoming you upon your arrival.

John Crowley
Partner
Coastwise Shipping Company

Courtesy of the Peabody Essex Museum, Salem, Massachusetts
The S.S. Philadelphia carried Captain Dow from Southampton to New York

I sit on my bed and ponder the logistics of making my way back home. I suppose I could leave as soon as next week. How to get to Southampton? With these ribs and my wrist, it's a good thing I'll be traveling light. I do think John is right to offer compensation to the Hicks, though I question whether they will accept. They are generous folk and see this hospitality as their Christian duty.

This schedule means I'll miss the presentation of honors to the crew of the *Slippen* by U.S. Consul Hooper. It's just as well. I've expressed my thanks and admiration to Freddie and Israel. That should suffice.

January 23rd, 1908

This last week has been rather active for a convalescing old codger such as me. On Tuesday, I visited Hughtown, on St. Mary's Island. I was able to visit the bank and a clothier, and have now returned all the borrowed clothing of the last six weeks. The trip on the ferry was such a joy—to be out on the water, feeling the roll of a deck beneath my feet. I hadn't realized how much I missed it. Walking through the town, seeing schoolchildren and shoppers in the streets, taking lunch at the local pub—all these remind me of the normal life that I have lacked since departing Marcus Hook last November.

Today looks like it's going to be beautiful, if cold. Good weather for a second visit to Hughtown. But this time, I won't be on the return ferry. Rather, I will be setting off for the mainland. It is early now as I wash, shave, and dress for the day of travel. I can hear Charlotte bustling about in the kitchen, fixing breakfast, and putting up a lunch that I will carry on my journey.

As I enter the kitchen, my dear hostess stops and appraises my appearance. "Very nice, Captain Dow, very handsome in your new suit and tie. You'll be the most distinguished passenger for the mainland, I'm sure. Now sit, sit. I've made scones this morning. They're Israel's favorite, though usually I don't make them unless the children are home."

I make appreciative sounds and inhale the aroma coming from the oven. As I pour my tea, Israel joins us. I know he has been up and out since before dawn and is just now returned. He offers a grunt of greeting and joins me at table. When the scones are set before us, his mood appears to brighten a bit.

"So it's off today, is it? Expect you'll be glad to be shut of St. Agnes after these long days.…"

"Oh, I wouldn't put it that way," I retort. "But it will be good to get back to Boston and my family. The people of St. Agnes have treated me well. I'll have some good memories of my stay here."

Charlotte joins us, and breakfast proceeds more in the manner of the dinner meal: the three of us are sitting down together, talking, and enjoying more than the usual morning fare.

"The scones are delicious, Charlotte. I must tell Jennie about them."

"I'll make a note of the recipe for her," she replies and hurries off for paper and pencil.

"I'll help you down to the ferry, Mr. Dow. Though your bag is light, it will still tax you, given that bad wrist."

"That's very kind, Mr. Hicks." I stand and brush a few crumbs of scone from my vest. "I'll be ready to leave in about fifteen minutes."

I make my way back to Rowe's room and knock. He's awake and dressed, seated before the breakfast tray prepared for him by Charlotte.

"Well, Captain, ready to cast off? Sure wish I was going with you. Folks in Wiscasset will think I've turned limey, decided to stay on here for good!"

I extend my left hand, which briefly perplexes him. He sets down his cup of tea, laughs, and grasps my hand awkwardly.

"I'll telephone your family once I'm home, Mr. Rowe. We'll not leave them in suspense as to your progress."

"Will you seek another command, Captain?"

I sigh and look out his bedroom window. He has a good view of Middle Town. "I will. It's a little late in life to be taking up a new line of work. And I'll need the money for the landlocked days ahead. How about you? Does the sea still call?"

"I don't know, rightly. I'll wait and see how these knees heal. I'm not afraid, mind you. Just want to know what my limitations will be."

"Ayah. That makes sense. Well, Rowe, best of luck. I wish you a speedy recovery and a safe journey home. When you're in Boston, ring me up and let me know how you've made out."

"Goodbye, Captain."

I detect him tearing up a bit—not for my taking leave, I'm sure, but for his staying behind. I walk back to my room and collect my things, few as they are. When I appear in the parlor, a visibly upset Charlotte is there.

"Oh Captain Dow, what foolishness for me—to be sad on what, for you, must be a happy occasion."

She forces a smile and hands me the note on scone making. I notice it is wet where a tear or two have fallen. The wrapped lunch is placed in my bag. I'm ready to go. All the words of thanks and good wishes are voiced again—redundantly, but necessarily. Israel takes my bag, and I don my new hat and coat.

"Goodbye, Charlotte. Don't take in any shipwrecked sailors for awhile."

She gives me a hug and retreats to the kitchen. Israel and I step out into the bright, crisp morning. The ferry can be seen rounding the edge of Gugh. Good timing.

The walk down to the quay is made without further conversation. When we arrive, I position myself apart from the others awaiting the ferry. I'm determined to leave Israel as best as I can manage. We stand, watching the ferry approach; then I break the silence.

"Look here, Mr. Hicks. I want you to know that I join you and your family in mourning Billy Cook. Believe me, I was powerless to save the *Lawson* and those aboard that night."

His face tightens; his eyes squint. Clearly I have touched the offended nerve. He removes his cap and scratches his scalp.

"Mr. Dow, I figure you're a sincere man. I take you at your word. Billy and I were best friends. It's going to take more than a few weeks for me to deal with his being gone."

I begin to formulate words of understanding and comfort. But before I can do so, he continues.

"I've thought this through, over and over. Here's how I choose to think about it. I've been on or about the water all my life. Frequently, I spend my spare time fishing. When I haul in my catch, I throw back almost half of what's in the net."

"Ayah, what we Yankees call the small fry."

"Correct. They get thrown back because they've got more growing to do. I believe you and I are still here for the same reason. We've both got more growing to do. But Billy, when he chose to go aboard the *Lawson*, it was to try to save that ship and her crew. It seems to me, at that moment, he showed himself fully grown and ready for taking."

Good God! This fellow has been thinking, and in ways I would not have guessed. I am rendered speechless. I nod my understanding just as the ferry lets out a blast from its steam whistle and pulls alongside the quay. As men toss lines and tie up, the small cluster of passengers edges forward.

"Mr. Hicks, thanks again. God bless you and yours."

He smiles, nods, and hands me my bag. Then he offers, for the first time, "Farewell, Captain."

Balm of Gilead!

Author's Note

If you enjoyed reading *Leviathan's Master*, please visit its page on Amazon.com and contribute your comments for the benefit of others who may also enjoy reading it.

Glossary

Abeam – at right angles to a ship's length or keel; abreast the middle of a ship's side

Balm of Gilead – any of several plants of the genus *Commiphora,* esp. *C. opobalsamum* and *C. meccanensis,* which yield a fragrant oleoresin. Also called Mecca balsam. The resin itself, a turbid yellow, green, or brownish-red, water-insoluble gluey liquid, used chiefly in perfumery. The phrase as used here is a popular oath of the nineteenth century.

Bowsprit – a large, tapered spar projecting forward from the bows of a sailing vessel

Cat-o'-nine-tails – a whip made of nine knotted cords attached to a handle, used for flogging

Collier – a ship for carrying coal

Coming about – see "tack"

Coxswain – the leader of a boat's crew, usually acting as helmsman

Davits – a pair of uprights that can be swung out over the side of a ship for lowering or raising a small boat

Deep-sea lead – a weight for measuring the depth of water at sea

Ditty bag – a small bag used by sailors for holding sewing equipment to repair sails and rigging

Dogwatch – either of the two duty periods aboard ship (from 4 to 6 p.m. and 6 to 8 p.m.), which are half the length of a normal period

Dory – a flat-bottomed rowboat with high, flaring sides, used chiefly in commercial fishing

Draft – the depth of water that a vessel draws or needs in order to float, especially when loaded

Expansion trunks – an appendage section of a liquid cargo carrying tank, typically positioned directly atop and forward of the main body of the tank; not only used to allow for gas expansion but also to reduce sloshing movements of liquid cargo

Fo'csle – familiar form of forecastle—the forward part of a vessel, below deck, where the sailors have their living quarters (pronounced fok-sil)

Free board – the area of a ship's side from the main deck or gunwale to the waterline

Gale force – a range of wind speed from thirty-two to sixty-three miles per hour, according to the Beaufort Scale

Gig – a long, light rowboat employing multiple rowers

Heave to – to put a ship into position to end forward progress

Knots – any of the knots tied at regular intervals in a log-line used in measuring a ship's speed, each equating to one nautical mile per hour

Limey – slang term for "British"

Log – any of various devices, originally a quadrant of wood, for measuring the speed of a ship; a drag mechanism attached to the end of a log-line; a log-chip

Lose way – to lose forward momentum of a ship

Luff – to turn the bow of a ship into or near the wind, a maneuver for heaving to

Mackintosh, or Mack – a waterproof outer coat

Mal de mer – French term for "seasickness"

Mizzenmast – the mast third from the bow in a ship with three or more masts

Oilskins – outer clothing made waterproof by treatment with oil

Overhang – the part of a ship's stern projecting beyond the sternpost

Rigging – the general term for all the ropes of a vessel; the ropes and other gear used to position, support, and control the masts, sails, yards, etc., of a sailing ship

RNLI (Royal National Lifeboat Institution)—a charity that saves lives at sea around the coasts of the British Isles, as well as inshore. It was founded on March 4, 1824, as the National Institution for the Preservation of Life from Shipwreck, adopting the present name in 1854.

Scale – the Beaufort Scale; see "gale force" above.

Sou'wester – familiar for southwester: a sailor's waterproof hat, the brim of which broadens in the back to protect the neck

Soundings – measurements of water depth taken at sea with lead weight and line

Spanker – the after mast and sail of a schooner-rigged vessel

Spoke – to have verbal communication between ships at sea

Steerage way – forward momentum of a ship sufficient to allow effective steering

Stud-link chain – chain fabricated such that each link is provided with a re-enforcing span or stud

Tack – to change the course of a sailing vessel by turning its bow into and across the wind; the opposite of wearing

Tacking – to tack, to sail against the wind by a series of tacks

Taking the sun – to fix a ship's position by use of a sextant, measuring the angular distance of the sun

Trinity House – The Corporation of Trinity House is the official General Lighthouse Authority for England, Wales, and other British territorial waters (with the exception of Scotland, Northern Ireland, and the Republic of Ireland). It is responsible for the provision and maintenance of navigational aids such as lighthouses, light vessels, buoys, and maritime radio/satellite communication systems. Trinity House is also the official Deep Sea Pilotage Authority providing expert navigators for ships trading in Northern European waters. It is a non-departmental public body (NDPB).

Warp – a rope used to move a vessel from one place to another, where one end is made fast to a fixed object

Wearing – to turn a vessel round, carrying the stern around by the wind

Wheelhouse – a pilothouse; ship's structure housing the steering wheel and providing shelter to the pilot or helmsman

Bibliography

American Lloyd's Register of American and Foreign Shipping, Record of American and Foreign Shipping, The Mystic Seaport, Museum of America and the Sea. Mystic, CT (www.mysticseaport. org).

Bunting, W.H. (ed.). *Portrait of a Port: Boston, 1852–1914*. Cambridge, MA: The Belknap Press of Harvard University Press, 1971.

Clapp, Edwin J. *The Port of Boston*. New Haven, CT: Yale University Press, 1916.

Crabtree, Alfred B. & Martin, Hattie B. *Hancock 1828–1928*. Augusta, ME: Kennebec Journal Co., 1928.

Dana, Richard Henry, Jr. *Two Years Before the Mast*. New York: Random House (Modern Library Paperback Edition), 2001.

"Disaster at Scilly." *The Western Weekly News,* Plymouth, U.K. December 21, 1907 (reprinted in *American Neptune,* April, 1969. Peabody Essex Museum. Salem, MA).

Dow, Scott J. *Captain Jonathan Dow: The Seafaring Days of Our New England Family*. Pasadena, CA: Scott J. Dow, 1948.

Duncan, Roger F. *Coastal Maine: A Maritime History.* Woodstock, VT: The Countryman Press, 1992.

Hall, Thomas. *The T. W. Lawson: The Fate of the World's Only Seven-Masted Schooner.* Charleston, SC: The History Press, 2006.

Henderson, Richard. *Hand, Reef, and Steer (revised)* Chicago: Contemporary Books, Inc., 1978.

Herbert, John R. *Thomas W. Lawson, Seven Masted Schooner. Mast Magazine,* August, 1949. United States Maritime Service, Washington, D.C.

Hornsby, Thomas. *The Last Voyage of the Thomas W. Lawson.* Cuba, NY: *The Nautical Research Journal.* April, 1953 (Nautical Research Guild).

Moon, T.C. *Untitled Article.* Ellsworth, Me: *The Ellsworth American,* August 4, 1926.

Paine, Lincoln P. *Down East: A Maritime History of Maine.* Gardiner, ME: Tilbury House, 2000.

Port of New York Passenger Records, The Statue of Liberty-Ellis Island Foundation (www.ellisisland.org).

Ronnberg, Erik, A. R., Jr. *Stranger in Truth Than in Fiction: The American Seven-Masted Schooners.* Cuba, NY: *The Nautical Research Journal* (Nautical Research Guild).

Rowe, William Hutchinson. *The Maritime History of Maine.* Gardiner, ME: The Harpswell Press, 1948.

"Schooner Lawson Wrecked; 16 Drown." *New York Times,* December 15, 1907.

"The Severe Gale; Many Lives Lost." *The Times,* London. December 16, 1907.

Snow, Edward Rowe. *The Sinking of the Thomas W. Lawson.* Boston: *Sunday Herald Traveler Magazine,* January 9, 1972.

State Street Trust Co. *Some Merchants and Sea Captains of Old Boston.* Boston: State Street Trust Co., 1918.

Wasson, Samuel. *Survey of Hancock County.* Augusta, ME: Sprague, Owen, & Nash, 1878.

Watts, Simon. *The Thomas W. Lawson: First or Last of the Great Sailing Bulk Carriers?* Peekskill, NY: Sea History, Winter, 1980. National Maritime Historical Society.

WPA Federal Writers Project *Boston Looks Seaward: The Story of the Port, 1630–1940.* Boston: Northeastern University Press, 1985.

"The Wreck off Scilly." *The Times,* London. December 17, 1907.

It May Be Forever—An Irish Rebel on the American Frontier by David M. Quinn

It May Be Forever is a nineteenth-century tale of adventure and tragedy based upon the real-life story of Michael Quinn. To escape the grinding poverty of Ireland's Great Famine, Michael and his family flee to England, where, at age eight, Michael becomes a child laborer in a textile mill. As he grows older and more aware of British prejudice and discrimination, he is motivated to enlist with the Fenian rebels, a group determined to free Ireland from British colonial rule. Chronic unemployment, however, drives him to America, and defeat on the battlefield lands him on the untamed plains of the Wild West.

Faced with unaccustomed opportunity, Michael quickly abandons the fight against oppression and turns away from family and friends. Dreams of achieving a great fortune lead him to support the dispossession of Native Americans of their lands and livelihood. But after the massacre at Wounded Knee, demons of conscience rise up in terrible nightmares, and only a Lakota holy man offers the hope of redemption.

It May Be Forever is a cautionary tale, which shows how the many small decisions of life can create the most unintended consequences and how easily a man of strong convictions may become that which he hates.

What reviewers are saying about *It May Be Forever:*

"Master storyteller, David Quinn, erases time…. To transport the reader is the writer's job. Quinn does just that."

Mary Sojourner, novelist of the Southwest

"What's unique about this biography turned novel is the real-life information threaded throughout like golden wire. It's obvious that Quinn has done his research to breathe life and breath into

Michael Quinn's tale.... I recommend David Quinn's book as an excellent and pleasurable way to learn your Irish and Irish American history. It's a gripping journey, colored with much tragedy and sadness, but excitement and joy as well. I thank David Quinn for sharing it with us."

Janet McGrane, CelticReader.Com

"The author invested considerable time in research, and the scenes depicted have a truly authentic ring.... David M. Quinn has succeeded in constructing a tale that links the sufferings of the Irish famine to those of the Native Americans at Wounded Knee. It is also a tale with a tentatively happy ending, an end to a life of bitterness but a life of extraordinary adventure peopled with extraordinary characters."

Pauline Ferrie, EmigrantOnline.ie

"The story is moving and compelling.... We are reminded who we are as a country and where we have been."

Jack L. Kennedy, Joplin Independent

Awards

Best Books Award Finalist 2006: USABookNews.com
Finalist — National Indie Excellence 2007 Book Awards
Arizona Book Publishing Association — Best First Book
(Honorable Mention)

Visit the author's website: www.itmaybeforever.com

Breinigsville, PA USA
31 August 2009
223287BV00001B/1/P